Oral
Anxiety

A Woman's Battle
With Her Sexual Demons

Photo Credit: © Can Stock Photo Inc. / mocker

ISBN- 13: 978-0692495148
ISBN-10: 0692495142

Printed in the United States of America.

Forelsket Press • Las Vegas, Nevada

Also by J.W. Richard

Crossed Signals
One Couple's Journey of Sexual Discovery

A Cougar Falls
Stunning Consequences

The Roles We Play
A Spank-tacular Tale

Sex is really only touch, the closest of all touch. And it's touch we're afraid of.

– D. H. LAWRENCE, *Lady Chatterley's Lover*

Chapter One

He stopped at the curb as his head swiveled both ways scanning for signs of trouble. Sensing no danger, he ran quickly across the street reaching the sidewalk in a few seconds. Safely on the opposite side, he stayed in the shadows as he moved along the chain link fence, came to the gate and slipped into the yard. His eyes scanned the lawn in front of him as he moved up to the nondescript ranch style house and stealthily made his way around to the back of the house. From the front he had seen the faint glow of a light from inside the house; as he reached the rear he saw that the light was from a rear room and he took care to stay in the shadows. He slowly weaved his way around clay pots and gardening tools carelessly strewn about being careful not to make a sound.

Somewhere in the distance a dog barked. He took one more look around before attempting to cross the last ten feet to safety. In a few quick strides he reached the side of the house and jumped up on the cinderblock and then the top of the garbage can and peered in the corner of the window. The shade was drawn but not all the way down and he still had a clear view. The eyes peered inside and followed the figure as it moved across the room seemingly unaware of his presence.

*****

She entered the room wearing a plush, white terrycloth robe, her hair wrapped in a towel. She moved across the room to her dresser, opened a drawer and took out a pair of flannel pajamas, tossing them on the bed. She went to the kitchen and filled the kettle with water, placed it on the stove and lit the burner. She set out her cup and placed a teabag in it and while she waited for the water to boil she went into the living room to find the magazine she'd bought earlier that day. By the time she returned to the kitchen the water was boiling so she filled her cup and returned to the bedroom.

She set the tea down on the table next to her recliner and turned on the reading lamp, then went back into the bathroom and removed the towel from her head and shook out her hair. After combing it she returned to the bedroom, loosened her robe just a little and sat down. She settled in to the chair and put her feet up on the footrest and opened *Cosmopolitan* and started thumbing through the pages until she found the article she wanted, the one she'd bought the magazine for – "Using Touch to get in Touch with your Sexuality." She started reading while sipping her beverage.

She finished the article, drained her tea and set the cup down on the table beside her. *Bat-shit crazy, but what the hell.* Settling back further into the chair her hand reached inside her robe at chest level as she started to lightly touch her breasts. A moment later she tossed the magazine aside and closed her eyes and in one motion flung the robe open and threw her left leg over the arm of the chair. Her fingers moved to the triangular patch of hair between her legs and worked gently through her pubes. Her fingertips traced her labia before slowly separating them. She moistened her right index finger and returned it to her clits and started rubbing lightly.

She felt only the softest of tingles so she used her left hand to massage her nipples. That was a little better. She slipped her finger inside her vagina and felt herself moistening just a little as the feeling started to intensify. She opened her eyes and watched as she mover her finger over and around her clit. She tried moving the way it was described in the article. It wasn't happening for her. She stood up and tossed the robe aside.

"What a load of crap."

She moved to her dresser drawer and retrieved her vibrator and sat back in the chair. She switched in on and held it against her clit and soon had a small, though not very satisfying orgasm. She put the vibrator away and moved to the bed to put her pajamas on. As she was stepping into the bottoms she heard a crashing noise that seemed to come from the backyard. She shut off the lights and finished dressing in the dark before peering out the window.

*****

The garbage can toppled over with a crash. The startled critter scampered away as fast as his four legs would carry him. He ran back out the front yard and across the street to safety not slowing down until he was several blocks away.

Chapter Two

Kellie was up much earlier than she needed to be having slept fitfully. The noise the night before spooked her. She masturbates so rarely and the sound she heard from outside her window seemed like a sign that she shouldn't have been playing with herself. She thought she had seen a shadow moving across her yard but when she turned the bedroom light out to get a better look she saw nothing. She went to the front of the house and looked out the window but didn't see anything there either. She assumed it must have been the wind or an animal but she made sure the doors and windows were all locked. As she tried to sleep the slightest noise startled her back awake. She still hadn't gotten used to living alone even though Chet had moved out almost three months ago.

Before getting ready for work, and still in her robe, she went out the back door and into the yard. She looked around and realized she hadn't been out there since Chet left. Signs of him were everywhere. Material and tools for the unfinished project he was working on were spread around the yard. The area had been dug out and the ground leveled, sand was piled in one corner, pavers stacked in another. Cinderblocks were placed around the edges of where the patio was going to be and several were stacked in front of the windows to her bedroom and the bathroom. A wheelbarrow was tipped on its side and next to lay a pair of work gloves. She righted the wheelbarrow and picked up the gloves, holding them gently as tears filled her eyes. *Why did it have to be this way?*

Tossing the gloves into the wheelbarrow she went back inside. Kellie had removed signs of Chet from the house interior but now realized how she had avoided dealing with the outside of the house. A thought occurred to her, could he have been in the yard to retrieve something the night before? He might have tried to do so quietly because he didn't want to disturb her at that time. She grabbed her phone and tapped out a text but stopped when she realized he wouldn't have been there so late.

She dressed for work in her typically conservative pantsuit, put on her makeup and was out the door with time enough to stop for a Starbucks on her way. Driving to work she pondered why she left the yard in such disarray. She concluded it was her secret hope that Chet would come back but she knew that wasn't going to happen. He was with someone else now who would give him what she couldn't – or wouldn't. She had to get on with her life and she would start by cleaning up the yard. She would have to hire someone because she couldn't do it herself but she had no idea who to call. She pulled into the parking lot of the insurance company and went in to her office.

After a couple of hours dealing with payables, receivables, and sending out reminders for past due invoices Kellie went to the break room for some coffee. She was still troubled by the previous evening and decided she would add a security alarm to her to-do list. She had her phone and looked at the text draft she hadn't sent and was about to delete it when the office sales manager walked into the room.

"Morning Kellie"

"Hi Steve, how's it going?"

"Same as always, you?"

"Dull and duller with a side of boring."

"My offer stands – dinner and drinks."

"So does my denial. I don't date guys I work with. Besides, you're ancient."

"Ten years older than you is not ancient."

"Thirteen."

Steve smiled. "So you've been checking, I'm flattered."

Kellie felt herself turn crimson. She had checked his file the first time he asked her out. He was forty-two, widowed, with a teenage son. Steve had briefly played professional football but a knee injury ended his career almost as soon as it started.

She found him attractive but just wasn't ready for a relationship with anyone, let alone a guy with a kid. She quickly changed the subject.

She had an idea. "Your son, uh..."

"Jason"

"Jason, does he do odd jobs?"

"Only for pretty women who date his father."

"Not happening."

"How about lunch in the break room?"

"Deal"

"What do you want done?"

Kellie explained what she needed and Steve said would have Jason stop by after school. They only lived a couple of blocks apart so he should be able to check out the project in the next day or so. She would have to negotiate the terms with Jason. Steve got up to leave but turned back to her.

"Did anyone ever tell you that you looked like Jini Meyer?" he asked.

"No, who the heck is Jenny Meyer?"

"Jini, Jini Meyer. She's a German rock singer."

"You listen to German music?"

"Jason does, he's taking German in school, says music helps him learn."

Kellie finished her coffee and went back to her office and the pile of accounting crap that awaited her return. She ate lunch at her desk, as she usually did on a Friday, she wanted her work to be finished so she could start the next week fresh. While she was eating her salad she surfed the net a bit. She googled "Jini Meyer" to see what would pop up. The results included text, presumably in German, that she couldn't read but there were several images. She clicked on one to enlarge it and it brought a smile to her face. *He thinks I look like her?*

She was in a great mood the rest of the day. She almost forgot about the night before but when it was time to go home for the day the memory of that noise returned. Not wanting to be alone, she called her sister but only got her voicemail. She left a message asking her if she could come over for a little while after work. She assumed Tracie would be going out as usual to do things she didn't care to think about but hoped she could swing by even for a short time. She really wanted a glass of wine but didn't like to drink alone and she certainly wasn't going out to a bar by herself. At five o'clock, her work done, she packed up and left.

Chapter Three

The wooden paddle swooshed through the air and came down on the reddened, bare ass with a resounding *thwack*. A stifled moan followed the sharp intake of breath. The paddle rose, paused, and came down again and again. Tracie saw her phone light up and was glad she remembered to set it to silent. She raised the paddle and delivered another blow as her eyes read the caller ID. Her attention turned back to her task with one last strike to deliver. She put all of her strength into it as the wooden implement crashed violently against the skin for the last time. *Thwack!*

"Ow!"

The recipient of her punishment had curled into a fetal position and was whimpering with tears flowing. Tracie stood up and circled around him, her stilettos clicking on the hardwood floor. Her boobs jiggled in her lace bra as she walked to the sofa and sat down.

"Mommy doesn't like to punish her little boy but you were bad. Do you understand that?"

"Ye...yes ma'am."

"You know you shouldn't play with your tiny pee-pee. You won't do that again will you?"

"No...no ma'am."

"Good boy. Now come to mommy."

Tracie sat back in the couch and opened her arms wide. Her "boy" stood up, all six foot two, two-hundred-fifty pounds of him. He snuggled into her as she put her right arm around him. Her left hand freed one of her boobs.

"Suck nice on mama's tittie."

As he suckled as if breast feeding her hand reached for his erect cock and stroked it until he shot a load across her bare thigh a minute or so later. She pushed him off her boob.

"You made a mess. Lick it up or you'll get another spanking."

He dropped to the floor on his knees and licked the semen from her leg. When he was done her hand cradled the top of his head and her fingers intertwined with the hair as she pulled him between her thighs to her shaved pussy.

"Now eat mommy good!"

He was licking and away and chomping on her a little too hard at times. After a few minutes she made her legs quiver and faked an orgasm. She pretended to catch her breath and pushed him a way.

"That's a good little boy. Now it's time for you to go home."

He got up to get dressed. When he turned away from her she saw the redness of his ass and smiled at her handy work. He couldn't eat pussy worth a damn but he could take a spanking better than any guy she knew. He said goodbye and left and as soon as he was out the door she retrieved the message from her sister then returned the call.

"I'd love to come over for some wine."

"Cool. When you didn't answer I figured you were already out for the night."

"No, I was just spanking a friend."

"I'd like to think you're joking, but knowing you..."

"You eat yet? I can bring takeout."

"Great idea. Surprise me but no Mexican this time."

"Done. See you in a few...open the wine."

Tracie stopped at Chinese restaurant and picked up several dishes they could share. She was glad Kellie called. Her sister hadn't been the same since she broke her engagement with Chet. Though she tried, she couldn't get Kellie to go out and have any fun and was starting to worry about her. Her sister was plain vanilla compared to her and knew she didn't approve of her sexual tastes or antics but she was still her sister and wanted her to be happy. An hour later she was at Kellie's door.

Chapter Four

Kellie reached for the takeout container with the sweet and sour pork and spooned some on her plate and added a helping of fried rice. Tracie got up off the floor and went to the kitchen coming back a moment later with refilled glasses of red wine. She handed one to Kellie before sitting back down at the coffee table. They had eaten Chinese food this way since they were kids and, as adults, never broke tradition by sitting at a table.

"This is so good," Kellie said. "Great idea."

"Merlot certainly helps – I needed this tonight."

"I'm glad you could make it. I thought you would probably be out at one of your orgies."

Tracie laughed. "There not orgies, they're called munches, and there's no sex involved. It's just a bunch of like-minded people getting together for drinks, food and conversation."

"Sort of networking for perverts," Kellie snickered.

"The term is 'alternative lifestyle,' not pervert."

"I don't know how you do all that fetish stuff."

"Said the church lady to the vanilla flock..."

Kellie chuckled and shook her head. It was hard to believe that they were children of the same parents. She was short, naturally blond, petit and very reserved and thought sex was something you only did with someone you were committed to and it certainly didn't involve any of the kinkiness her sister enjoyed. Tracie was tall, dark-haired, with the build of an Amazon woman complete with huge boobs that she loved to show off. Sex for her sister was a form of recreation, not an expression of love. She jokingly called herself a tri-sexual because she'll try anything. The thought of the things her sister routinely did were repulsive to her. Despite being opposites in almost every way they were incredibly close and Kellie loved her and loved being with her.

"I'm not vanilla, I just have morals."

"Fuck morals, I'd rather have fun."

They finished their dinner and both of them got up to clear the remnants of their feast and clear way the dishes and empty cartons. They moved to the kitchen where Kellie loaded the dishwasher as Tracie refilled their glasses. They continued their conversation as they leaned against the kitchen counter.

Kellie sipped her wine. "You weren't really spanking someone, were you?"

"Damn straight, they don't call me 'Madam

Spanks-a-Lot' for nothing."

"You're too much. Guys really like that?"

"More than you could possibly imagine. A lot, and I mean really a lot, of guys crave discipline."

"It seems so strange."

"Come to one of my dungeon parties and you'll see."

"Thanks, but I'll pass. It's too weird for me."

They moved back into the living room with glasses refilled from a newly-opened second bottle of wine. Kellie was feeling more relaxed than she had been in a long time. They talked about their jobs and what was going on in their lives. Eventually Tracie moved the conversation to a subject that Kellie wanted to avoid.

"Have you dated anyone?"

"You know I haven't," Kellie said.

"No one interests you at all? You know what they say, when you fall off a horse..."

"No, I'm just not ready. There is a guy at work who's been after me but he's too old and has a kid."

"So. The older the violin, the sweeter the music. Besides, kids grow up eventually."

"He's a nice guy and all but I'm just not interested. Though he does think I look like some German rock star."

"Do you? Look like her, I mean."

"I googled her. We have the same build and hair style but she's gorgeous."

"Have you looked in a mirror lately? So are you."

"C'mon, I'm a bag of bones and I've got these little flap-jack boobies." With that her hands brushed at her breasts making them jiggle a little. "Now if I had hooters like yours..."

Tracie stood up and shifted her ass toward her sister and gave it a smack. "And I've got a huge ass to go with them."

"A big booty is the in thing today."

"Thanks to J-Lo and Kim-K. I'd much rather have a championship-quality derriere like yours."

"No way," Kellie laughed. "Without that caboose for ballast you'd keel over from the weight of your tits."

They both laughed until tears were flowing, each feeling the effects of the wine.

"Hey, I know," Tracie said. "We'll combine assets. Your ass, my boobs..."

"Your height..."

"And your face. We'll put Kate Upton to shame!"

"Why not your face? You're pretty," Kellie said.

"I do admit that I'm beautiful," Tracie said with a laugh, "But I've got this pig nose, not a classic Greek one like you."

"One thing for sure," Kellie said, "Our 'Tra-Kellie' goddess has to have your sex drive, giving it mine would be a total waste of such a gorgeous creation."

Kellie's expression suddenly changed to one of sadness. She went quiet as she sipped her wine and her eyes moistened. Tracie noticed and put her glass down and took her sisters hands in hers.

"Hey, what's wrong?"

Kellie shook her head and freed one of her hands to wipe her eyes. "It's nothing."

"Bullshit," Tracie said. "Missing Chet?"

Kellie looked up at her sister. Tears welled up and began to flow down her cheeks. Her lip quivered as she shook her head affirmatively as she began to bawl. She felt her sister's arms go around her and pull her close. Her head nestled in Tracie's bosom, she began to convulse as she sobbed loudly.

Lying in bed later that night, and feeling the effects of far too much wine, a kaleidoscope of thoughts and jumbled emotions coursed through her brain. She started thinking of Chet as her hand slipped inside her panties, a moment later she was flinging the underwear across the room. Several minutes passed before she gave up in frustration and reached for her phone.

Chapter Five

He watched the red strands of hair as her head moved side to side slowly, then up and down. She made a light slurping sound as she worked on his cock. She took a deep breath then slowly took him all the way in her mouth and came back up slowly with her tongue moving along the shaft applying pressure as she moved. Her mouth came off his penis and moved to his balls, taking them in her mouth one at a time biting lightly, then sucking hard. He inhaled sharply as she took him back in his mouth. When he was ready to explode she came off again with her fingers wrapped around him and squeezing. She had an amazing ability to keep him right on the edge.

She looked up at him. "God I love your cock! Now give me your cum."

She went back down on him and he exploded into her mouth. She sucked on him until every last drop was emptied. She looked up at him again and opened her mouth to show him the load of semen on her tongue, then she swallowed it and climbed up and cuddled against his chest.

She nibbled on his ear lobe. "That was *sooo* yummy. Now eat my pussy."

She sat up and threw one leg over him and straddled his chest. He put his hands on her hips and guided her up toward his face. His eyes fixed on the narrow strip of orange-red pubic hair as she moved her very wet vagina to his waiting mouth. His tongue found her clit and she moved a bit as he licked her. In a matter of minutes she was moaning and she pulled his head in tight. He was having trouble breathing when she suddenly convulsed and shuddered.

"*Aghhh!* Oh yes! God yes!"

She slid down off of his mouth and onto his chest. Her hand reached behind her and found his semi-erect cock. Her hand tugged on it at it stiffened a little. Still holding it and tugging, she slid down until her pussy was just above it. Still not fully hard, she started shoving it inside her. He helped her as he grew just hard enough and she started sliding up and down and he finally became fully erect. Her hand grabbed his and pulled it behind her ass. He knew what she wanted so he brought his hand to his mouth and moistened his fingers. He moved back down and her hand grabbed him again to hurry him along. His wet finger located her anus and found its way inside.

"Ahh yes! Fuck me...fuck both holes!"

She was panting hard as he synchronized his hand movement with her gyrations. She was bucking wildly and gasping then stopped suddenly and moved off him. She faced away from him on all fours.

"Fuck my ass – now! Hurry!"

He came up behind her on his knees. Her hand reached around and grabbed his cock, guiding it to her ass. She pushed against his cock as he pushed into her. After a moment's resistance he slipped inside of her and started pumping.

"Hard...fuck me hard...that's it. Oh god, harder!"

Their skin made a slapping sound and he slammed against her. Her ass was in the air, her head buried in the pillow. She was fingering herself the whole time. She started breathing heavily and cried out. As her body shuddered in orgasm he came inside her ass. They collapsed in a heap, she was facedown with him on top of her, his cock still in her ass. They both caught their breath and his penis slipped out of her as he went limp.

"That was...that was awesome," she said. "Nobody's ever fucked me like you do."

Chet sat up and reached for the water bottle on the night stand. He took a drink before handing it to Jean. She took a big gulp and handed it back. He screwed the cap back on the bottle and put it back. As he did he saw his phone light up indicating he had a text. He glanced at the time on the alarm clock – 3:27AM – as he picked up the phone to read the message. It simply said "miss u."

He set the phone down and snuggled into Jean's back pulling her close and spooning her. She murmured a soft good night as she closed her eyes. His were wide open as he thought about the woman who had never come remotely close to fucking the way Jean just had. He missed her too.

Chapter Six

A freight train rumbled through her head as her temples pounded. Kellie resisted the urge to heave up last night's dinner as she made her way to her bathroom. She slowly sat down on the bowl and held her head in her hands as she peed. She sat there for several minutes after she was done, afraid to initiate the vertigo that would surely accompany standing up. Finally rising, she stood at the sink and rinsed her face with cold water and stared at her ragged reflection.

"Had to have that third bottle, didn't you?"

She was going back to the bedroom when she heard a noise from the kitchen and remembered that Tracie, far too drunk to drive home, was spending the night. After she recovered from her emotional breakdown they spent the rest of the night talking and drinking, drinking and talking. Kellie didn't recall much of their conversation and she wasn't sure what time she finally went to bed, she just knew that it was very late. She saw her panties lying on the floor against the wall as if they had been flung there. Puzzled at first because she usually slept with them on, she recalled doing something else she very rarely did – trying to masturbate. She brought her fingers to her nose and sniffed catching the remnants of her own scent and realized she must have fallen asleep while doing it. Feeling steady enough to join her sister, she started for the door.

"Well good morning sunshine," Tracie said as she put a cup of coffee down in front of her sister.

"Why aren't you as hung-over as I am?"

"Because I puked my guts up last night after you went to bed. Trust me, I feel as shitty as you look."

They sat there quietly slowly eating English muffins and sipping their coffee. Kellie saw her sister looking at her as if she wanted to say something.

"What?"

Tracie cradled her cup. "You said something last night that I didn't understand."

"Maybe because I was three sheets to the wind?"

"No, I'm serious," Tracie said. "You said it was all your fault but you wouldn't explain. What really happened between you and Chet?"

"It was my fault and I *don't* want to talk about it."

"C'mon sis, you can talk to me. You can't hold it in. What did you do?"

"It's what I didn't do."

"Huh? What didn't you do?"

Kellie felt the blood rushing to her head and her hands began to tremble. She clenched her teeth, picked her cup up and slammed it back down with enough force for the coffee to erupt and spew over the table. Tracie was startle by her reaction and stared at her wide-eyed.

Kellie took a deep breath and through clenched teeth said, "I wouldn't suck his cock, ok? Happy? I wouldn't put his goddamn dick in my little prude mouth and he left me, okay?"

"Easy girl. You were together for three years, you never gave him a blowjob?"

"Never."

"Why did it take him so long to realize that was a deal breaker?"

"He thought he could deal with it at first. About a month before we broke up he asked me to at least try but I refused. Then he said he couldn't live the rest of his life without it. I told him he was welcome to get it from someone else but I wasn't doing it."

Tracie shook her head. "Why did it take a month for him to leave?"

"He thought I was serious when I said to get it somewhere else, maybe I was...I just don't know anymore. He went out with his buddies one night and when he came home he was acting weird. I pushed and pushed until he told me that he got a blowjob from a hooker."

"But you told him to."

"I know, but we still had a huge fight and that was it. He moved out the next day."

"Sis, I'm so sorry."

Kellie wiped a tear. "And that's the story about how the prude fucked up the best thing that ever happened to her."

Tracie poured more coffee for both of them. She found some fruit in the refrigerator and set it on the table with a couple of bowls and spoons. They dug in quietly for a long while before Tracie spoke again.

"I'm sorry Kellie, but I'm having a hard time comprehending. I love sucking cock."

"But aren't you afraid they'll...you know...do it in your mouth?"

Tracie laughed. "Honey, if I do all that work they damn well better cum in my mouth. I love the taste of semen and I want every last drop."

Kellie shuddered. "That's gross."

"Why is it so gross? Didn't you ever try it?"

Kellie hung her head and her expression changed. Tracie waited patiently determined not to say another word until her sister did. After almost ten minutes Kellie looked up at Tracie.

"Remember the family barbeque at Aunt Charlotte's when mom and dad had that huge fight?"

"God, that was what? Ten, twelve years ago?"

"Sixteen."

Chapter Seven

"Sixteen years ago?" Tracie said. "Are you sure?"

"I know for sure, I was thirteen."

Kellie stopped speaking again, lost in her thoughts. Her sister wanted to say something but waited, impatiently for sure, but waited. Kellie shifted in her seat, started to talk, stopped, then finally started again after clearing her throat.

"Do you remember what mom and dad were arguing about?"

"I'm not really sure, I just remember being glad it had nothing to do with me."

Kellie sat up straighter. "They were arguing about me because I was piss-assed drunk."

"That's why you were asleep the whole way home."

"I embarrassed the crap out of them and they were arguing about whose fault it was. They each said the other should have been watching me. Then they blamed me because I should have known better."

"Why were you drinking anyway and how did you get the booze?"

Kellie sighed. "Remember our cousin Travis?"

"Oh yeah, I thought he was so hot. If you were thirteen, I was fifteen. He must have been about twenty-one or two. I remember he acted like I didn't exist. What about him?"

"He gave me the booze."

"Travis?"

"Uh huh. Gave me a weird tasting drink and said to give it a try. I didn't really want it but I was trying to impress him. Being around him made me feel funny, I know now it was the hormones."

"How many did you have?"

"I don't know, but when I finished one he got me another. I remember feeling different."

"What happened?" Tracie asked.

"He asked if I wanted to take a walk and get away from the party."

Kellie lost herself in the recollection.

She was walking down the street with Travis. As soon as they were out of sight of her aunt's house he took her hand. She felt a strange tingling between her legs. They walked to the local park and sat on top of a picnic table, their feet on the benches. She was feeling a little woozy, so when he put his arm around her she rested her head on his shoulder. He shifted and brought his lips to hers and kissed her. It was her first kiss. She enjoyed it until he tried to push his tongue in her mouth.

Kellie pushed him away. "What are you doing?"

"Haven't you ever French kissed?"

"Um...yeah, sure."

Travis laughed. "Come here, let me show you. Open your mouth just a little."

She parted her lips and closed her eyes. His lips softly touched hers. His tongue slowly entered her mouth and found hers. He moved it around and she willingly accepted it. There was a strange sensation in her groin and she felt herself getting moist. Her breath quickened a little as he caressed her back. She heard a soft moaning sound and realized it was coming from her. This seemed to go for hours but was really only a few minutes. His free hand slipped under her shirt and cupped her bra and rubbed her beast. She knew she should stop him but didn't. Apparently emboldened by her lack of resistance, Travis moved his other hand from her back and started to lower the zipper of her jeans. She quickly sat up and pushed him away.

"No!"

"I'm just trying to make you feel good."

"I feel good."

"Then you can make me feel good."

They resumed kissing. She was puzzled. *Didn't he feel good kissing her?* When he tried to slip his hand under her shirt she stopped him this time. As her hand was pushing his away he held it and guided it down to his crotch and pushed it against him. She paused as she felt a large bulge but soon pulled away from him. He pushed her hand back. She wanted to pull away but was curious and allowed her fingertips to feel the outline of his penis, at least that's what she assumed it was. Confused, she again pulled away. Travis sat back with a frustrated look on his face.

"Are you some kind of tease?"

"What? Huh? No...I mean..."

"What?"

She didn't want to upset him. "I just...I never touched one before."

He smiled. "Really? I thought a pretty girl like you would have been with plenty of guys."

Kellie felt her face flush as she turned crimson. *Pretty? He thinks I'm pretty?*

Travis stood up and reached his hand out. She took it and jumped down off the table. He guided her away and toward the tree line.

"Where are we going?"

"Over here where no one can see."

Though not sure she should, she followed him behind some bushes. They stopped at a small clearing; he sat her down on a tree stump and stood in front of her. Alarm bells went off in her head when he started to unbuckle his belt but she was unable to move. With a mixture of fear, curiosity and excitement her eyes fixed on his zipper as he lowered it. Her mouth dropped open as he pushed his jeans lower exposing himself. Though she knew how it worked, to this point an erect penis existed only in the chattering of adolescent girls. Now a hard cock throbbed mere inches from her face.

Travis took her hand and pulled it toward him. "Go ahead, touch it. See what it feels like."

Her fingers tentatively caressed the shaft, it was amazingly soft. She touched the head a moment then he took her hand and guided it toward his testicles. Her eyes never left his cock as her fingers examined him. He had her wrap her fingers around it and move up and down.

"That's it. That feels good."

Travis steadied himself by placing one hand on her shoulder. She looked up at him, his eyes were closed and he seemed to be miles away. She was getting into a rhythm but her hand was getting tired so she stopped. He opened his eyes and moved closer to her face; she instinctively pulled back but he just moved closer.

"Kiss it," he said.

Kellie did as he asked and pulled back again.

"Now lick it, go ahead, lick it."

She licked the head quickly and tasted something salty with a sticky consistency. She pulled away once more though her hand didn't let go of him.

"That's it. Now suck on it."

"What?"

"Put it in your mouth."

"Huh? No."

"No? I thought you were a woman, all women do that."

Still quite drunk, and wanting him to think she was grown up, she put the head in her mouth.

"That's it, now take it all the way."

She went a little more and felt the urge to gag.

"Easy, go slow. You're doing real good."

She tried a little more and was starting to back away again when his hand grabbed the back of her head. She tried to pull off him but his grip was to strong. He pushed his cock in deeper and she had no choice but to open her mouth. She couldn't breathe as he started pumping faster. He stiffened and grunted and she felt something hot shooting into her mouth as his penis pulsated. He finally stopped and she pushed him away. Bent over with her hands on her knees she was retching as she spit white goo out of her mouth.

Wiping her lips she glared at him. "What the fuck were you doing?"

"Showing you how to give a blowjob but I guess you're just a little kid after all."

She started storming away. "I'm telling my parents what you did."

Travis caught up to her and walked next to her. "Go ahead, nobody will believe you. They'll just think their little girl is a slut."

She walked back to her aunt's house with tears streaming down her face.

Tracie sat there looking at her. "That little prick. He's a child molester and he raped you."

"Now do you understand why I won't suck cock?"

"Yeah, but sis, you should have told someone."

"I believed him when he said they would blame me."

"You could have told me, I would've believed you."

"I know that *now*," Kellie said. "I had no idea what was happening when he came in my mouth, I didn't know that dicks ejaculated."

Tracie took her sister's hand and squeezed. "I can't believe what he did to you. Did you ever try to suck after that?"

Tears streamed down Kellie's face. "I...I couldn't. Whenever a guy pushed for it I broke up with him."

"No wonder you kept ditching guys, I just thought you were super picky. So Chet didn't try?"

"He did once, but when I told him I wouldn't he didn't push until that last time. He seemed perfectly happy as long as I gave him a lot of hand jobs."

"So you were okay with jerking guys off?"

"I was with Chet, we usually made a game of it."

"How so?"

Kellie started to laugh and wiped her eyes. "We did it in the strangest places. He'd say, 'here's a good spot' – that was our code word – and I'd make him cum. I never wanted to tell him 'no' because I wouldn't do what he really wanted."

Tracie shook her head. "You surprise me, maybe there's hope for my little prude sister yet. What were some of the strange spots?"

"Some you'd probably guess, like the movies. I did it in the car a lot. We'd go to a friend's house and I'd do him before we went in. I did him at a drive through while we were getting takeout burgers, the dressing room of a department store, the beach, your bedroom."

"Wait, what? You did him in my bedroom?"

"Uh huh, when you had us over last year."

"You little bitch, the least you could've done was let me watch!"

Chapter Eight

He was facing the Saint Andrews cross, arms and legs making an "x" as he was stretched out and secured by the restraints. His bare ass was glowing red from the paddle blows, his cries muffled by the ball gag strapped to his mouth. His head was straining in an effort to see behind him, his eyes wide and watery as he awaited the next strike. A hand grabbed his hair and twisted it around so he was facing the forward. A blindfold was slipped over his head and the strap tightly secured.

"You know you weren't supposed to peek, Kyle," Tracie said. "For that you're getting five more."

Kyle whimpered as she delivered another hard blow. *Whack!* The paddle made a sharp sound against the bare skin as his body shook. He tensed for another strike but she made him wait as she circled around him. She liked Kyle. He was about forty-five, in great shape with nicely toned and well-defined muscles. She looked at his cock which was perfectly situated just below the intersection of the wooden boards where they formed the "x."

Rigidly at attention when the session began, his penis now hung limp. She finished her circle and delivered another blow. *Whack!* She delivered two more, slightly lighter in force, and began to circle again. She knew he was waiting for the last one and by now he would want it to be over. She made him wait.

She walked over to the bench that contained assorted "goodies" being sure that her stilettos clicked loudly on the tile floor. She found what she was looking for and selected one that was medium in size. She applied a liberal amount of lubricant and walked back over to Kyle. She saw droplets of sweat appear from under the blindfold and trickle slowly down his face. He was trembling in a combination of fear and anticipation – just the way she liked it. She circled him three more times before she lifted the paddle above her head and delivered the most forceful blow yet. *Whack!*

Arrgghhh!

She grabbed the bright-red left cheek of his ass and roughly spread it, digging her long nails into the flesh as she did so. She located his anus and swiftly inserted the lubricated butt plug as far as it would go while Kyle let out a muffled groan. She moved on to phase two.

She pulled a chair over to the opposite side of the cross and sat down facing his cock. It was one of her favorites. About eight inches long when erect, it was circumcised and perfectly shaped. It started coming to life as soon as she touched it. She lowered her mouth to it and licked and kissed it until he was better than halfway up. She took it in her mouth and worked it slowly until he was fully hard. She fondled his balls while she sucked, giving an occasional firm squeeze to remind him who was in charge – as if he didn't already know.

Tracie stood up and discarded her panties and kicked them across the floor. She leaned forward slightly and backed into him. Her hand reached around and grabbed his cock as she moved slightly until she felt it against her pussy lips. *Like docking with the Space Shuttle*. She was already soaking wet; she practically had an orgasm from spanking him. She pushed back until he was fully inside her and she felt him straining to thrust but that was just about impossible with the restraints. She rocked slowly until she found her rhythm and then picked up the pace. She was starting to breathe heavily and felt her orgasm building when she heard him grunt through the gag and she felt the pulsation from his cock and the warmth of his semen as he ejaculated.

She pulled off of him, went to the other side of the cross and undid the gag, then the restraints as fast as she could, legs first. He flexed his arms to restore the circulation as she released him from the bindings.

"You bastard, I was almost there. On the floor! Now!"

Kyle got on his back as she straddled his face, his semen dripping down on him as it oozed out of her vagina.

"Eat me damn it!"

She felt his tongue on her clit as he skillfully brought her back to the edge of orgasm. Of all her playmates he ate her best and he wasn't disappointing her now. She squirmed on his face as she began to lose control. Her legs began to quiver and the rest of her trembled as a jolt of electricity coursed through her.

Ahh! Ahhh! Oh Yes! Urghhh! Ahhh!

Tracie collapsed on his face and quickly rolled off. She pulled Kyle up to her and he began to lightly suck on her nipple as she recovered and her breathing returned to normal. When she was back under control she got up and went to the kitchen. She returned a few minutes later with a couple of beers and a bottle of lotion. She sat on the couch and motioned for him to come over and handed him a brew.

"Come here, baby."

She had him lay face down across her lap and she applied lotion to his cheeks. She saw the plug was still in his ass so she carefully removed it. He sat up and the silently drank their beers. When he was done he stood and got dressed while she watched.

Kyle came over and kissed her. "That was awesome, you're the best."

She smiled at him. "I certainly enjoyed it. You're a lot of fun Kyle, thanks."

After he left she folded the cross and wheeled it back to the closet. This session was just what the doctor ordered. She had recovered from her hangover by the time she went to her Saturday afternoon rope and bondage class. She certainly didn't need the instruction on how to safely use knots and restraints but she liked connecting with others from her circle. She ran into Kyle there. They had played together a few times before and he told her he was feeling a need for some discipline if she was in the mood. She readily agreed and was glad she had.

Kellie's revelation had upset her. Not just because of what happened, but because she could relate. She had her own incident when *she* was thirteen, though nothing like her sister's. It was with the older brother of a friend. She was at her girlfriend's house when the brother lured her into the basement on some pretense and tried to kiss her. When she resisted he pushed her to the floor; straddling her and used his knees to pin her arms. She was totally helpless as he controlled her and she remembered seeing a depraved look in his eyes that caused her to tremble in fear. Unable to resist him, he opened her shirt and fondled her boobs. Then he pulled her bra up to expose her nipples but that wasn't good enough. He reached around her back and tried to unfasten the clasp and that was her chance. She kneed him in the balls and pushed him off of her and ran up the stairs.

What troubled her was not the dredging up of a long-forgotten memory, but the meaning behind it. Her sister had been so traumatized that she was unable to perform oral sex. In her case it was where her need to dominate men came from. If she was in control of them they couldn't control her like her friend's brother had. Tracie feared she may have actually suffered more damage than her sister. Kellie couldn't suck cock but she had fallen deeply in love, Tracie couldn't get enough cock to suck but had never been in love with anyone.

Chapter Nine

For most people Monday existed as a day to dread. Their new workweek often began with the leftovers from the Friday before, incomplete assignments, ignored problems, or projects left for another day. Kellie operated in a different manner, her work never seemed to linger. She read somewhere long ago that the majority of stress resulted from unfinished tasks so she vowed to remain at least one step ahead of her workload whenever possible. She typically attacked her week with gusto, rapidly annihilating the to-do list she created each Friday afternoon. Today wasn't such a day. Her anxiety needle pinned the redline after a weekend spent ruminating over the disaster of her failed relationship. Rather than helping, talking with Tracie pulled everything up to the surface again.

Shortly after arriving she buried herself in a stack of reports and worked her way through it without pause until lunchtime arrived. She debated going out for a bite or ordering in from the deli that delivered every day. The deli won since she had little desire to leave the office. She rummaged through her desk drawer for the menu when her intercom buzzed.

The receptionist's voice came over the speaker. "Kellie? Steve is ready for you in the break room."

"Huh? Oh shit, I'll be there in a minute."

Her promise to Steve totally slipped her mind. She stashed the menu back in the drawer and placed the reports in a neat pile. She reached under the desk for her shoes and slipped them back on. People flashed sly looks and assorted smirks as she strolled past. She reached the break room door and found in a position she'd never seen before – closed. Puzzled, she reached for the door handle and noticed a note that read, "Private meeting in progress." She hesitated briefly before entering, reacting in surprise as she did so. The lights were off with only a small amount of sunlight peaking in through the closed blinds. A lone table, draped with a white tablecloth and lit by two candles, occupied the center of the room, the others moved off to the side.

Leslie, the office receptionist, looking very formal with a small, white towel draped over her arm, stepped from the shadows and motioned for her to be seated.

"Steven will be joining you momentarily."

She let out an amused laugh, her dark mood lifting. The door opened and Steve entered wearing a black tuxedo. He walked to the side of the table and bowed in greeting. Leslie stepped over and pulled out his chair then retreated to the far end of the room as he sat down. She caught the smell of Italian food and realized she was famished.

"This is nuts," Kellie said.

"Perhaps, but it's as close to a real date as I'll ever get so I wanted it to be memorable."

"The office will be talking about this," she said with no effort to disguise her concern. "They'll put two and two together and come up with the wrong answer."

"Fear not, my dear. I made it quite clear what was going on so they'll be no untoward gossip. Now the tabloids on the other hand..."

She laughed again as Leslie placed their dishes in front of them. Plates of veal Parmigiana with sides of spaghetti filled the table. They both dug in with gusto and she needed to remind herself to slow down. They talked about inconsequential things and laughed a lot until they were both finished. Leslie cleared the plates and Steve's expression turned serious.

"Jason will be over this afternoon after school," he said.

"I'm looking forward to it."

"Well, there is something you should know. He's had a hard time since his mother died."

"That had to be rough," she said, "on both of you."

"He has a hard time relating to people, especially women. He pretty much keeps to himself and, frankly, I'm concerned. The counselor says he'll get through it but I don't know, it's been almost five years now."

Kellie noticed the tears welling up in his eyes. She reached for his hand, which was resting on the table, and covered it with hers. He looked directly at her.

"I just wanted you to know, in case he seems weird."

"You're a good dad."

At home after what turned out to be a very interesting day, Kellie got out of her dress clothes. She walked around her bedroom wearing only her panties while hanging up her pantsuit. The ringing of the doorbell startled her but she quickly realized Jason was coming over. Muttering an "oh, shit," she grabbed a long, very loose-fitting t-shirt and rushed to answer the door. She opened it to find a rail-thin, scraggly-haired teenager of medium height standing there with his eyes averted.

"You must be Jason, hi."

"Hello Ms. Boyd."

"Call me Kellie. Come on, I'll show you what needs to be done."

She stepped out the front door and walked around toward the back yard with Jason following behind her. Without pants on she felt a bit self-conscious and hoped the neighbors weren't looking, though the shirt was more than long enough. Kellie realized the shirt was one of Chet's which explained why it was so big on her.

In the back Kellie pointed out the areas she wanted him to straighten up and told him where to put things. They discussed how he might get rid of piles of dirt and sand and possible places to stash the cinderblocks. She explained that her goal was for everything to be neat and that he should use his own discretion. Jason walked around the yard checking things out for a few minutes.

"So that's the job," she said. "How much do you want to do it?"

"Whatever you want to pay me is fine, Ms. Boyd."

"Kellie, got it?"

"Yes, Ms...Kellie."

They walked back around to the front with Jason following a step behind and to the side. She glanced back at him and he quickly looked away and she thought she saw him blush. She remembered what Steve said and assumed he was just feeling a bit awkward. Jason said he would be back the next afternoon to get started and walked away as she went inside.

Kellie walked back to her bedroom and as she was passing her mirror she stopped. She looked at herself as she slowly turned to the side and realized what Jason was looking at and why he blushed. The t-shirt was so oversized that the armholes billowed open when she turned a certain way providing a fairly decent side-boob shot.

Well Steve, seems your boy is a little more normal than you think.

Chapter Ten

The sparse crowd at the bar was fairly normal for a Monday night considering it wasn't football season. The greatest concentration of customers occupied the small, semi-private room toward the back. Tracie sat at a pub table with Cheryl, a woman friend, having a drink and scanning the people as they rolled in for the weekly munch. She found amusement in watching the newbies, especially men, crash and burn. They usually stumble across the *Fetlife* website, find out about the munch and expect to walk in and get laid. The guys will invariably create a user name containing the obligatory "wolf" and proclaim themselves to be "Doms" thinking that women will do whatever they say. After approaching a few veteran "subs" who promptly put them in their place they wind up leaving with their little wolf-tails between their legs. Naturally not all of them were like that and Tracie met a number of fantastic playmates at some of these gatherings. Of course those guys knew what the meets were really for, getting to know other members and not an event for hooking up.

"So I have this idea for a scene," Cheryl said. "Well, it's partly Daryl's idea."

"Let me guess, it involves me," Tracie said.

Cheryl smiled. "Of course, you know he loves your ass – and everything else."

"But he's got such a tiny dick."

"I know, that's what makes him so much fun, I love humiliating him."

"What is he, like three inches if that?" Tracie asked.

"Four and a half, but it's so thin and his big balls make it look even smaller."

Tracie finished her drink and signaled the waitress for another. Cheryl asked her to play a couple of times before but she always turned her down. She and Daryl really got off on the humiliation play but it didn't do much for her. They did have some contact in group scenes which was how she knew about her man's miniscule member. She could see that Cheryl was really excited about whatever they were planning so she'd at least hear her out. The waitress returned with drinks for both of them.

"So what's your scene?" Tracie asked.

Cheryl took a sip of her drink. "Imagine a doctor's office – we have a real one we can use – Daryl comes in for an exam, you're the doctor and I'm the assistant."

"Okay so far."

"I tell him to get undressed and he does, except for his underwear. You come in and examine him and tell him to bend over and give him a rectal exam by pulling his underwear down over his butt cheeks but not all the way. Then you tell him to remove his briefs so you can check for a hernia but he refuses."

"Sounds fairly normal so far."

"I'm getting to the good part. Since he won't cooperate we tie his wrists to the bed to restrain him. Once he's secure I pull his underwear down and you start laughing at him because he's so small. Then you tell him he needs to be punished for not obeying. We bend him over the table and you spank the living shit out of him as only you can do."

"That part sounds like fun," Tracie said.

"There's more. After the spanking we make him watch while I go down on you."

"You know I'm not into women."

"I know," Cheryl said. "But I am and you can pretend. At least one of us will enjoy it. To end the scene and really humiliate him we'll make him lay on the floor and I'll piss in his face."

Tracie was thinking of a polite way to say "no" when she blurted out, "Okay, I'll do it."

She wondered if she'd done the right thing but she didn't back out after giving her word. She knew this was really for Cheryl, her friend hinted many times that she wanted to fuck her and even asked her directly at least once. They were discussing the logistics of day and time when a familiar face walked in. The woman, Jean, was a group regular but not one that Tracie ever crossed paths with. It was the guy she was with that surprised her – Chet.

She watched them walk to the other end of the room, greeting several people as they went. They seemed to be heading to a specific couple and she saw she was right when they joined the pair at their table. Jean was a bisexual kinkster who had a reputation of doing just about anything with anyone at anytime. That's why she was astonished to see Chet with her because he seemed so straight-laced. Or was she simply projecting her sister's demeanor onto him? Maybe Chet was kinkier than she assumed.

Tracie excused herself from Cheryl and headed to the ladies room. Instead of returning to her chair she stayed at the bar where she had a view into the room and could easily observe Chet, Jean and the other couple. After several minutes Jean turned to Chet and gave him what appeared to be an icy glare but she wasn't certain. Chet stood up and was shaking his head as if he didn't agree with something. Jean stood as well, grabbed her purse and seemed to be saying goodbye to the other couple. Then she turned and walked quickly toward the door, looking really pissed. Chet was right on her heels.

As they passed the bar Chet turned to her – he obviously knew all along that she was there. He held two fingers to the side of his face in a universal sign while he mouthed the words "call me." She had no idea what it was all about but she was curious as hell.

Chapter Eleven

Kellie dealt with a few snickers and suggestive remarks on Tuesday, but it was all in fun. Steve wasn't kidding when he said he made it clear that there was nothing going on between them. She settled into her day and things moved along without anything more than the usual minor glitches and complications. She saw Steve only briefly but told him everything was set with Jason and that she thought he was a normal kid. She didn't tell him just how normal he was by peeking at her boobs. Of course, she thought it was really her fault because she shouldn't have been dressed that way.

She arrived home that afternoon and found Jason hard at work in the yard. She stuck her head out the back door and offered him a drink but other than that she stayed out of his way. The last thing she wanted to do was hover over him and cause him feel nervous, besides he probably had a better idea of what to do with the yard than she ever would. She left an extra can of soda on the steps and went back inside.

Kellie went in to her bedroom and took off her blouse and slipped on a t-shirt – hers this time with her bra still on. Still wearing her skirt, she hung up the dry-cleaning she picked up on her way home. She retrieved her jeans from the closet and was about to put them on when she heard a knock from the back door. Jason was standing there holding his work gloves so she motioned him to step inside.

"It's getting dark, I'll finish tomorrow."

"That's fine Jason."

"Ms Bo...Kellie, do you have a key to the shed? It's locked and I want to put the tools away."

Kellie thought for a moment. "I must have one somewhere, hold on."

She looked on top of the refrigerator and then the table by the door – nothing. She looked around the kitchen and went to her junk drawer. She rummaged through it but couldn't find anything. She pulled the drawer out all the way and took it to the table. Pulling up a chair, she sat down and rifled through the contents. Within a few seconds she found the keys and held them up in triumph. She looked up at Jason and blushed when she realized her legs were spread wide and he was staring right up her skirt.

She stood up and handed him the keys but told him to leave the stuff where it was for now. It had been there for months and another day wouldn't matter. Jason took the keys and left. Kellie took the kitchen chair into her bedroom and set it down in front of her full-length mirror. She sat and spread her legs trying to figure out what Jason saw. Her white lace panties were clearly visible with the dark outline of her pubes. Then she wondered if he even knew what pubic hair was since all girls seem to shave these days. *Kellie, what are you doing to this poor kid?*

Chapter Twelve

The car pulled into the driveway and Chet looked at Jean. She stared out the window after not uttering a word for the entire ride. He knew she was pissed but didn't really care. He shut the car off and walked toward his front door, she finally got out of the vehicle slamming the door behind her. He went inside without waiting and went straight to his bedroom and changed into his sweats. When he came back to the living room he saw her standing by the door, arms folded across her chest obviously ready for a fight. He sat without a word and turned on the TV, totally ignoring her.

She marched over and stood between him and the television. "You humiliated me in front of my friends!"

"Friends? Or fuck buddies?"

"They're both. I should have known you couldn't handle it."

"I can handle it, just not what they had in mind," he said.

" *You* said you wanted to do it with another couple but when I set it up you back out."

"First – it was your idea. Second, I would fuck another woman but I'm not giving a guy a blowjob or letting him fuck me up the ass like he wanted to."

That's how a real foursome works. It's okay for me and her to do it but you won't fuck him?"

"I'm not gay!"

"Neither am I," she said.

"So you're bi."

"No, I'm heteroflexible. If it feels good I'll do it, I don't care if it's a guy or girl."

"Call it what you want."

She stormed to the door and stood there facing him. "I thought you were cool. You have a nice dick, but you're a real asshole."

"Fuck you."

"Not anymore you won't." She walked out slamming the door behind her.

A sense of relief washed over him. Jean excited him and did things sexually he never imagined were possible. He just wasn't ready for her world nor did he imagine he ever would be. He knew from the beginning the relationship wouldn't last but he did have fun until now. The best thing that happened tonight was seeing Tracie, he'd wanted to talk to her for some time but was reluctant to call her. Hopefully she would reach out to him now, if she didn't he would call her.

Chet went to the kitchen and grabbed a Sam

Adams out of the fridge. He sat back on the couch and started channel surfing. He settled on a sitcom, put the remote down and picked up his phone. He opened the text screen and read her message yet again – "miss u" – and was tempted once more to respond. He didn't because he knew nothing would change. He switched to the "pictures" screen and started scrolling until he found several of Kellie. He found the one he was looking for, the one she didn't know about because he snapped it while she was sleeping. She looked so innocent yet incredibly sexy. She was sprawled on the bed on her side – nude – her right breast partially obscured, the left one fully visible. Her gorgeous pussy with the lush patch of dark pubic hair was perfectly clear and he imagined himself eating her. He slipped his cock from his sweats and stroked himself until he exploded.

Chapter Thirteen

The pot of stew simmered on the stove as the aroma of baking biscuits wafted through the kitchen. Steve stirred the pot and shut off the gas. He was removing the biscuits from the oven just as Jason walked in. He filled two bowls and set them on the kitchen table as Jason was talking off his jacket and hanging it up on the hook behind the door.

"Just in time," Steve said. "How did it go?"

"Okay, I have to go back after school tomorrow to finish up."

Jason didn't offer anything else and sat there eating his dinner. Steve watched him as he ate from his own bowl. He asked him a couple of questions about the job and a few more about school and received the typical short answers. He knew part of this was just his son being a teenager. Jason did well in school and wasn't a problem in any way, he just wasn't much for conversation. What really worried Steve was that he just really didn't show much enthusiasm for anything, not outwardly anyway. Perhaps he was just naturally introverted.

They finished at the same time. Steve got up and put the empty bowls and spoons into the dishwasher as Jason wrapped up the leftover biscuits. Steve was scooping the remaining stew into plastic containers when Jason tossed something onto the counter.

"What's that?"

"Oh, Ms. Boyd's keys. I have to remember to take them tomorrow so I can get into the shed."

"Was it okay working for her?"

"Yeah. She's really...."

"Pretty?"

"Well, yeah, but I was going to say 'nice.' She reminds me of..."

"Jini?"

Jason paused a moment. "Mom...she reminds me of mom."

Jason left the room while Steve continued cleaning up. He heard the music go on in Jason's room, rock with lyrics in German that he couldn't understand. His son's words echoed in his head, Jason had never compared his mother to another woman before. Steve picked up the keys and held them in front of him. Tears came to his eyes as he realized that was the reason he liked Kellie so much himself. A sense of sadness enveloped him because he knew that was also why it could never work.

Chapter Fourteen

Several days passed and with each one Tracie agonized whether to call Chet. On Tuesday it was "absolutely not" because she didn't want to get involved in her sister's business. Wednesday she almost did since she knew it may be the only chance of them getting back together. Thursday morning she reverted to "no way" since it could backfire. Thursday afternoon she reached "fuck it" and dialed his number. He was glad she called and they agreed to meet at the bar that evening.

She dressed carefully since she didn't know what he wanted, though she guessed, and didn't want to take any chances. She was used to teasing him playfully and more than once caught him checking her out. It just proved he was human and he'd never given the slightest hint of being at all interested in her. All the same she made sure there was no cleavage, or anything else, showing.

She arrived at the bar early only to find that he was already there waiting and he stood to greet her as she walked to his booth. He had a half-finished draft in front of him so he'd been there at least a little while. He flagged down the waitress and ordered a drink for her and a refill for him along with an appetizer platter.

"How've you been?" she asked him.

"Truthfully, I've been better. You?"

"The same," she said. "I must admit I was surprised to see you, especially with Jean."

"I thought you might know her."

"How's it going between you two?"

"It's not, we broke up that night."

Tracie saw in his demeanor that he didn't seem too upset about it. "I'm sorry."

"Don't be, we had no chance. I knew that from the get go."

"How did you meet?"

"In a bar, I was just there looking for a burger and beer and we started chatting. One thing led to another and the next thing you know..."

"She did you in the bathroom."

Chet's jaw hung agape. "She told you?"

Tracie laughed. "No....that's how she usually picks up guys. Wants to find out right away if the, um, 'measure up' and know how to fuck. If they can't handle it she's not interested. I guess you passed the test."

Chet shook his head. "Wow. Well, I shouldn't be too surprised though; I can't handle her world."

She looked into his eyes. "I take it you didn't want to see me to talk about Jean."

"No, no I didn't. How is she?"

"She's hurting."

"I thought so."

"How would you know? She says you haven't talked since you...since the breakup."

Chet fumbled with his phone then handed it to her. She looked at the screen – *miss u* – then looked at the date and made the connection. She wondered if Kellie even realized she sent it.

"She was drunk."

"Are you sure? How can you tell?"

"I was with her that night, we both got trashed."

Tracie watched him as his thoughts obviously turned inward. She waited patiently wondering how far she should go. He was uncomfortable, that much was certain, but she could see he wanted to talk about it.

"Why don't you call her?"

"I...I can't. It wouldn't be fair to her. Being with Jean made it all too clear that I can never go back."

"Was sex with Kellie really that bad? Or was Jean really that good?"

"She did things I didn't know were even possible, but that's not it."

"Look Chet, I know Kellie won't suck your cock but she *loves* you. Don't you see that?"

A tear rolled down his cheek. "Of course I see that, but it's not enough. Yes, she won't do *that*, but..."

"Oh come on already, you're not twelve and I not Mother Theresa – call a blow job a blow job."

"Fine, she won't blow me, ok? That's still not what I'm talking about."

"What then?" she asked.

"Well that *is* a little of it, I'm not going to live the rest of my life without getting...without getting sucked off once in a while. But the thing is that Jean wanted me...she *wanted* me."

"Kellie wants you."

"No," he said. "Kellie loves me, she wants to please me, in her own way anyway. But she doesn't *want* me."

"I'm sorry Chet, I'm confused."

He took a large gulp and drained his beer and signaled for another. He ate a potato skin from the platter in front of him and wiped his mouth with a napkin before continuing.

"Let me try to explain. There are times when I look at her, Kellie, and she is just so damn sexy. I just want to rip her clothes off, bury my face between her legs and make her squeal and scream until she can't take it anymore. Of course that never happens, she's too reserved to let herself go like that, but that's how I feel and I make sure she knows it. She never feels that way about me, if she does she never showed it."

Tracie was at a loss. "I, I had no idea. I think she just isn't wired that way. I know she always wants to please you and does what she can. Thanks for getting jerked off in my bedroom by the way."

"She told you?"

"Yeah, the least you could do was let me watch."

He laughed. "That's exactly what I mean though. She 'takes care' of me but she doesn't *want* me."

"Did you ever say that to her?"

He shook his head. "No, but I didn't realize it myself until Jean. That's what's really been missing for me, though I still need the other thing."

Tracie didn't know what to say, she had no answer at all for this. Knowing her sister she could absolutely understand where he was coming from. She just told him to be patient and give Kellie some space and maybe things could work out. They finished the appetizers and drinks and left the bar. He walked her to her car and they hugged good bye. She had a thought and held the embrace a bit longer than necessary.

She spoke softly into his ear. "You know how much I love my sister, right?"

"Of course I do."

"Well understand this is for her. If you guys do get back together, and I really hope you do, you have a standing offer from me."

"Offer of what?"

"If you ever feel the need for a blow job and she won't do it, you can get it from me."

"Huh?"

"I'm dead serious. I don't want that issue to keep you apart. I'll suck you off, no questions, no judgments, and no one will ever know. Anytime you want."

"But..."

She put her finger to his lips to silence him. "Anytime. Trust me, I suck like a champ and I'm much better than Jean."

Her hand patted his crotch and was happy to feel a growing bulge. Message received. She left him standing there with a dazed look as she drove away.

Chapter Fifteen

Pavers were neatly stacked along one side of the yard. Cinderblocks were in three separate piles along the back of the house. Decorative rocks were not only spread out where they were designed to go, they had been used to cover the dirt area that had been leveled for the pavers. Tools were picked up and stacked neatly inside the shed and the assorted piles of dirt had miraculously disappeared. Kellie was beyond pleased, she was shocked; the yard had never looked this good.

She put her hand on Jason's shoulder. "This is fantastic. What did you do with the dirt?"

"I spread it out under the rocks."

"Unbelievable. Come on inside."

She went into the back door with Jason following behind her. She wasn't surprised that he was here, she expected it. What she didn't anticipate that he had been here for hours and finished the job with results that far exceeded her expectations. She was only looking to get the yard cleaned up. She told Jason to take a seat at the kitchen table and gave him a soda and asked him to wait a moment.

She went into the bedroom to get the envelope with cash she had set aside for him. She took another hundred from her purse and added it and considered it a bargain for what he had done. He was waiting patiently almost finished with his drink.

She handed him the money. "Thank you so much, you did a fantastic job."

He took the envelope and glanced inside. "This is too much."

"You said I could pay you whatever I wanted."

"Yeah but..."

She held up her hand. "No, you earned it so take it."

He stood up. "Thank you Ms. Boyd...Kellie."

"You're very welcome."

Jason left through the front and she closed the door behind him. She went in the bedroom and stripped of her pantsuit and blouse. She hung them up in her closet then took off her bra and went into the bathroom. Standing in front of the mirror wearing only her panties, she put her hair up in a ponytail. She was about to remove her makeup when the doorbell rang. Puzzled because she wasn't expecting anyone, she slipped on her robe and went to answer the door. Before opening it she glanced out the window and saw Jason, he must have forgotten something. She opened the door.

"Hi Jason."

"I...I forgot to give you these back." He held out her keys.

She reached for them and as she was taking them they slipped from her hand. She bent down to pick them up fumbling for a moment before grabbing them. As she started back up her robe billowed open fully exposing her right breast. She quickly covered herself but Jason had been staring right at her and she realized she had just given him another eyeful, nipple and all. His crimson complexion told her all she needed to know. He stammered a goodbye as she closed the door and leaned back against it letting out a deep breath. *He must think I'm some sort of cougar slut.*

The rest of the week she kept missing Steve at work somehow. She wanted to let him know how well his son had done but he never seemed to be around. She left him a note but never heard from him and began to wonder if he was upset with her for some reason. She hoped he didn't feel rejected after their lunch on Monday, she hadn't said anything that hadn't been said before. She really liked him, just not the way he wanted her to. By Friday she was thinking about sending him an email when she saw him walk through the hall and down to his office. She stopped what she was doing and went to see him.

She stood at his office door and waited for him to look up. "Got a sec?"

He looked up at her, his expression strange. "Sure, what's up?"

Kellie walked in and sat down. "That's what I wanted to ask you. I feel like you've been avoiding me all week, is everything okay?"

He looked at her a moment before speaking. "Between us, yeah."

She detected sadness in his eyes. "What's wrong? I'm your friend, you can talk to me."

He started to speak, then stopped. Kellie waited and he finally spoke. "Would you have a drink with me after work?"

She was surprised. "Steve, I told you I..."

"No, no...not a date. I'd just rather chat over a drink. Just one, I promise."

"Okay, one drink," she said. "I'll meet you at the pub by our house after work."

Back in her office she thought about it and wasn't sure she was doing the right thing. She picked up her phone and was about to text Tracie when she decided to call her instead.

Her sister answered right away. "Are you spanking anyone after work?"

"No why?" she laughed. "Have someone who needs their butt whacked?"

"No, I need a chaperone."

"God, you are a prude."

Kellie explained what she wanted and Tracie agreed to meet her at the bar at six. That would give her and Steve about forty minutes or so to chat. It wasn't that she didn't trust Steve, she did. She just didn't want to hurt him. She hung up with her sister and returned to her work. She moved her cell phone off her desk and saw she had left her text application open and went to close it. As she did so her eye caught something unusual. She opened the app back up and saw Chet's name. She went to the last message and saw it was from her to him. She read it, looked at the date and time, read it again.

"What the *fuck* did I do?"

Her horror turned to sadness when she realized he never responded.

Chapter Sixteen

The pub was starting to get busy with the after work happy hour crowd. Kellie made her way in looking for Steve. She was feeling a mixture of apprehension, concern and curiosity. She wanted to believe he was sincere when he said he wasn't trying for a date. Since he insisted he wasn't she was genuinely concerned that something was wrong and she hoped she could help in some way. She didn't see him when she started scanning the room but saw him walk through the front door a minute or so later. He spotted her and when their eyes met hers she pointed to a high pub table toward the back of the bar. He nodded his head and they converged on the spot.

They sat at the stools and Steve flagged down the waitress and ordered drinks for both of them and a plate of nachos. They made small talk as they waited for their drinks to arrive. In an effort to lighten the mood she made a comment about agreeing to a drink, but nachos were not a part of the negotiations.

"I thought you might be hungry."

"I am and it'll go good with my margarita...my *one* margarita."

The nachos arrived and they dug in. Steve still hadn't given her a hint of what was bothering him. She would wait a little longer for him to open up but she was serious about her one drink, though the nachos were good and hitting the spot.

"I don't know if Jason told you," she said. "He did a fantastic job."

"He only said you overpaid him."

"Trust me, he deserved it. He's a good kid."

"Thanks."

She was almost finished with her drink so she thought it was time. "So what's on your mind?"

He went quiet and hung his head. "I was thinking a lot, about us."

Kellie felt the hair on the back of her neck stand up. "Steve, I told you..."

He held his hand up. "No, no...it's not what you think. Please hear me out."

She sat back and waited. "Go ahead."

"I realized something, actually Jason helped me realize it. I've made no secret about being attracted to you. I even thought I loved you, now I realize why. You remind me of Sharon...my wife. I can't begin to tell you how much I miss her."

"Steve, I'm so sorry."

"No, it's okay. It's just that even if you did want to date me, and I know you don't, it could never work. I would always compare you to her and that wouldn't be fair. Not to you, not to me, and not to Sharon's memory. I...I just hope you'll continue to be my friend." A tear rolled down his cheek.

Her own tears were flowing and she made no effort to stop them. She got up off of her stool and slid over to him putting her arms around him and whispering in his ear. "Of course I will."

She held him for a moment as he wrapped his arms around her and returned her embrace. She kissed him on the cheek and pulled away, returning to her own stool. She dried her eyes as he did the same. As she was gathering herself she saw Tracie walk in and she waved in her direction. Her sister saw her and made her way over.

Tracie hugged her sister and looked at Steve. "And who's this?

"Tracie meet Steve, Steve meet my sister Tracie."

Kellie watched with amusement as the two of them appraised each other. Steve was eyeballing Tracie's cleavage, which was on full display, and Tracie was no doubt sizing up his "spankability" or whatever term she used. It was all she could do to avoid laughing out loud at the pageantry of the scene. After talking a bit Steve finished his drink, paid the waitress and said goodbye, keeping his promise of only having one drink. He left the remainder of the nachos for them to share. Kellie watched her sister as her eyes followed Steve until he was out the door.

"You bitch!" she said. "You didn't tell me he was a fucking hunk."

"You didn't ask."

"Did you see those pecs? Those biceps? Those baby-blue eyes? He is hot, hot, *hot*."

"I noticed the muscles. He used to play for the Raiders or Niners, I'm not sure which."

"Why the hell don't you go out with him?"

"Too late now, he just broke off the relationship we never had."

Tracie was understandably confused so Kellie slowly told her the whole story. By the time she finished she was drying her eyes once more and Tracie was dabbing at hers.

"What an amazing guy, romantic too. They don't make them like that anymore. At least I don't see them but they seem to gravitate to you."

"What good does it do? I can't keep them."

"You could if..."

"I know, if I learned to suck cock."

"It might be a little more than that."

"What do you mean?"

"I talked to Chet."

Chapter Seventeen

A tremendous weight lifted itself from Steve's shoulders. For months on end he'd been obsessing over Kellie, he assumed it was because she was she was pretty, smart and had a great personality. All it took was a simple comment from his teenage son to open his eyes to the real reason. For five years he had been unknowingly looking for a woman to fill the void in his heart and soul left by Sharon's death. In all that time he hadn't dated because no one measured up, that is until he joined the agency and met Kellie. He now realized he'd been pursuing a ghost, an unrealistic fantasy. He was finally ready to move on.

Though she didn't look exactly like his wife, Kellie did resemble her and was similar in build and temperament. It was her personality that had drawn him in and what his son had noticed as being similar to Sharon. Facing the reality that Kellie was a fantasy that would never happen allowed him to think of other women, one other woman to be precise. As he drove home he thought of how different Kellie was from her sister, he never would have guessed they were related. Tracie was much taller than Kellie, big-boned with large breasts and looked like she was well able to take care of herself physically. Though she seemed tough, Tracie still came across as feminine and sexy. Very sexy. Something happened to Steve that hadn't occurred in a very long time – he had a massive erection.

He pulled the car into the garage and headed inside. Fortunately his hard-on had subsided. Music was coming from Jason's room as he made his way to the kitchen. The remnants of a frozen pizza were on the counter, the carton sticking out the top of the trash. He pushed the box down into the can so the lid would close then placed the three remaining slices in the toaster oven to heat them up. The nachos hadn't been enough for dinner and he didn't fell like making real food. He was putting the now hot pizza on a plate when Jason walked into the room.

"I left it out because I thought you might want it, I wasn't expecting you to be late."

"I should have told you. I was out with Kellie."

"Kellie? Oh, Ms. Boyd. Out? Like a date?"

"No. Would that have been a problem though? Me dating I mean."

"No...no, it wouldn't be a problem. Why should it be?"

"Well, I haven't dated since...."

"Well maybe it's time you did," Jason said.

Steve felt even better. He certainly didn't need his son's permission to go out with women, nor was he seeking it, he just didn't want to upset him. He finished his pizza and Jason went back to his room. After changing out of his work clothes and into his sweats, Steve went to his home office and fired up his laptop. He navigated to Facebook and clicked Kellie's profile from his "friends" list. Once there he browsed through her friends until he found her sister and clicked on that profile. He read the "about" section then scrolled through her pictures. Before long his hard-on was back. Her "about" page had a link to a website called *Fetlife* so he clicked on it. Once there his erection started to throb with a vengeance – it was her profile page on a fetish website. He read the page, seeing the many things she was into and did something else he hadn't done in a while – he slipped his cock out of his pants and jerked off.

Chapter Eighteen

"When did you see Chet? Why didn't you tell me?"

"Relax," Tracie said. "It was yesterday and I'm telling you now."

The waitress brought over another round of drinks and cleared the plates from the nachos. Kellie couldn't believe her sister met with Chet without telling her first. She wasn't angry, just anxious to know what he said and what she meant by "more." Her mind was racing with a combination of anticipation and dread.

"How is he," Kellie asked. "How did he look?"

"He looks good but he's hurting too."

"Is he angry with me...does he hate me?"

Tracie let out an exasperated sigh. "Will you take a chill pill? God, he doesn't hate you. He loves you."

Kellie felt the tears welling up in her eyes. "But....?"

"Did you see how I looked at Steve?"

"Yeah, and?"

"What did I look like?"

"Like you wanted to rip his clothes off."

"Exactly."

"I don't get it, what's the point?"

Tracie took an audible breath before continuing. "When's the last time you looked at Chet like that?"

"What? All the time."

"Really? When did you ever look at him and want to rip his pants off to get your hands on his cock?"

"I played with it all the time."

Tracie shook her head. "That's not what I'm asking. When's the last time you just had to *have* his cock?"

She was confused. "I'm...I'm not wired like that."

"Exactly, that's the problem. Chet never felt like you wanted him."

"That's ridiculous, of course I wanted him."

"I'm not so sure," Tracie said. "Besides, the point is you never made him *feel* that you did."

"But I never said no to him."

Tracie sighed. "You're not understanding. All guys, even down-to-earth guys like Chet, have an ego that needs to be stroked. They need to feel wanted and that you can't keep your hands off them."

"He had to know."

"He knew, knows you love him. But you never made him feel it."

Kellie started to cry. She felt her sister's hand on her and then Tracie came over to her side of the booth and hugged her. She buried her face in her sister's shoulder and let the tears flow. After Kellie calmed herself Tracie moved back to her side of the booth.

"I still have a hard time believing he felt that way," Kellie said.

"What is his cock like?"

"Huh?"

"Describe his dick to me."

"Well, it's circumcised, and it's big..."

"How big? How many inches? Didn't you ever take a ruler to it? How thick?"

"I don't know – seven, eight inches. It's pretty thick, I can barely wrap my hand around it."

"What's the head like? Does it curve? Which way? What about his balls?"

"I don't know, how is this important?"

"Seriously? Even guys who have their head on straight are wrapped up in their penis. They don't call it their *manhood* for nothing. They need to be told how special it is and, more importantly, how much you *love* it."

She started crying again. "I just don't think like that. Maybe there is something wrong with me."

"You might be asexual," Tracie said. "More likely is that that prick Travis did more damage to you than you think."

"But it was so long ago."

"When you were just learning about sex," Tracie said. "Didn't you tell me you were really curious that day?"

"I guess."

"You wanted to see his cock, to touch it?"

"Yeah, so?"

"Have you felt that way since?"

"I...I don't remember...I don't think so."

Tracie sighed. "That's my point. You do everything you think you're *supposed* to do. But you do it like you're following an instruction manual instead of doing it because you *want* to."

"But I want to make him happy," Kellie pleaded.

"Making him happy is great, but you have to do it to make *you* happy, because *you* want it, because *you* have to have it."

Kellie choked back a sob. "I don't know how, damn it...I don't know *how*."

Tracie reached out and held her sister's hand. "You really need to talk to my therapist friend."

Chapter Nineteen

Naked, Tracie faced the mirror and tried to decide what to do. She hated the bald look because she was tired of looking like everyone else. That style stood out when few women shaved it but now almost all did so it was no longer unique. She decided to go for the Mohawk strip. She climbed into the shower and ran her fingers across her pubic stubble, then lathered up sitting on the edge of the tub. She carefully drew the razor across her skin being careful not to cut herself. When she was finished she showered and washed her hair.

Back in front of the mirror she inspected her handiwork and decided she'd made the right choice, now she just needed to wait for it to grow in. She hoped Steve would like it and quickly wondered why she cared. She had been thinking of him went she went to bed and, typical of nights when she didn't have sex, masturbating. He was still on her mind when she woke up so she started her day by vibrating herself to a nice orgasm. Masturbating a lot was certainly not out of the ordinary, repeatedly thinking about a specific guy was. She usually fantasized about certain acts such as sucking cock or giving a nice ass a good working over. Now she was fantasizing about *a* guy, admittedly a hot one but it was not normal for her. She absolutely needed to get laid before the day was over. She started thinking about who might be available for a play-date.

She scrolled through her phone's address book looking for a possible hookup when she spotted a name that made her stop. Kellie had only said she'd think about her offer and may never agree to go ahead but she thought she get the ball rolling anyway. She dialed the number and waited.

"Glenda," she said. "Can anyone really be asexual?"

"Well good morning Tracie. I get the feeling you aren't talking about you."

"No, it's...a friend."

"I see," Glenda said. "Is this, um, *friend* male or female?"

"It's a woman."

"How old?"

"Twenty-nine."

"Okay, now we're getting somewhere. It's a woman you know well enough to know her exact, rather than approximate, age. Hopefully you have other specific details as well. For instance, is she a virgin? Does she have any sexual feeling at all and has she always been this way?"

"She's had sexual relationships but sex is

meaningless to her. She does it to accommodate her partner rather than for her own pleasure."

"Okay," Glenda said. "Stop right there. I can't diagnose someone I've never met nor can I offer them advice. Speaking in general terms, some people are truly asexual. More often than not the real issue is some past trauma that impairs their ability to enjoy sex."

"Like rape or being molested?"

"That qualifies as trauma. But that may not be the case here and I really need to see this person to make that diagnosis."

"Understood. I'm trying to get her to see you. Thanks Glenda."

Knuckles turned white as the grip on the sheets tightened. On her knees, her ample breasts swayed like a pendulum with each thrust as his skin smacked loudly against her ass. She'd already had two orgasms but felt the big one building. The huge cock was gliding in and out of her soaking wet pussy and she knew by his grunts that he was getting close as well. She started getting light-headed and lowered her head, turned sideways, into the soft pillow.

Ahhh...ahhh...Oh yeah...ahhh....ughh ahhh!

Gasping for breath, Tracie spun around causing him to slip out of her. Her hand grabbed his cock and stroked furiously as she got into position. Her mouth found him just as he ejaculated with a loud grunt and she felt the hot semen hit the roof of her mouth. She greedily sucked out every last drop then they both collapsed in a heap on the sweat-soaked sheets.

"God, I needed that!" she said.

Will was a young guy about ten years younger than her but he had a great cock, knew how to use it and had great stamina. Perfect for when she needed a real pounding. He wasn't one of her regular spanking playmates. She had met him in a bar one night about a year before and they wound up in bed. Since then they had hooked up several times for a casual encounter like this one. He was the fourth guy she reached out to that afternoon but the first that was able to get together. She wasn't sorry.

Another great thing about Will – he didn't linger. About fifteen minutes after they were done he was dressed and out the door after telling her to call anytime because he loved fucking her. She jumped in the shower for a quick rinse, her vagina just a little sore and her nipples tender from his playful nips. She slipped on a pair of panties, put on her jeans and threw a sweatshirt, sans bra, over her head. After pouring herself a glass of merlot she settled down in front of the television. She clicked though the channels as thoughts of Steve popped into her head. *Damn!*

Chapter Twenty

Kellie tossed and turned all night. She even tried masturbating to help her doze off to no avail. Her sister's revelation upset her of course, but as she tried to sleep she kept replaying the conversation in her head her anxiety level ratcheted up several notches. She must have misunderstood what Chet was saying. He had to know how much she wanted him, couldn't he feel it? Tracie couldn't be right, she just couldn't. *Could she?* Recalling moments in her relationship with Chet convinced her that it wasn't that way. Then, staring at the ceiling, she pictured the alternative and concluded it *was* that way. *I'm a cold, dead fish.*

Saturday was normally an opportunity to stay in bed a little longer but her mind was racing so furiously that Kellie rose with the dawn to face the day. She started a pot of coffee and jumped in the shower while it brewed. She lathered up and ran her hands over her nipples looking for a reaction of some kind. They perked up right on cue but there was no jolt or sexual feeling at all. She moved lower and soaped her bush and rubbed her clit for a long moment. Nothing. *What's the matter with me?*

She toweled off, put on her favorite sweats and put her hair up in a pony tail. She took a quick look in the mirror. *I do look like that Jini person, too bad I can't sing.* She went into the kitchen and poured a cup of coffee and took it, along with her laptop, to the living room and made herself comfortable on the sofa. She started doing random searches based on what Tracie said the night before. She closed her eyes and the conversation with her sister played again and again as if on an endless loop. *Maybe I really am asexual.*

Tired of searching after an hour or so, Kellie closed her computer and switched on the TV. She surfed the channels until she found a romantic comedy and watched it without really paying attention. When it was over she came across another movie she hadn't seen in a while and watched that. By late afternoon she had accomplished absolutely nothing and didn't care. A thought occurred to her so she opened up her laptop again. She found a porn site and started searching. She wasn't looking to be stimulated, she was looking for something specific. She wanted to find a picture of a cock that looked like Chet's. It wasn't easy and she knew why. Tracie was right – in all the time they had been together and despite the dozens of times she had given him a hand job, she had never taken a good look at his penis. She examined picture after picture, hard cock and soft, but nothing struck her as being similar. She knew he was circumcised and pretty big but beyond that she would have a hard time describing the specifics. She looked at her hand and tried to recall how it felt as she held it.

Next she found a series of oral sex videos. She watched women sucking guys off, stared as they licked, slurped and sucked. If they didn't enjoy it they were great actresses. Not one of them showed the slightest apprehension at sticking the monster dicks in their mouth. She continued to watch as the guys came and the girls ate the semen, or let it shoot all over their face. *Why do detest doing that? Why is it so repulsive to me?*

Kellie paused the video and went into the kitchen and returned with a medium-sized cucumber. She restarted the video and mimicked the action on the screen using the vegetable. It didn't bother her at all but this a cold cucumber, it wasn't a warm, live dick attached to a real person. It certainly wasn't going to shoot a load of warm goo into her mouth. She put the cucumber down and looked intently at the picture as a guy shot his load all over the girls face. The actress smiled as licked as much as her tongue could reach, then used her fingers to scrape off the rest and licked that up too. Kellie shivered and almost retched at the sight. *I'm not normal, I need help.*

She picked up the phone and waited for her sister to answer. "Give me that shrink's number."

Chapter Twenty-One

All week long Chet mulled over what Tracie said that night. He knew she was dead serious but he didn't know how to take it. Was she really willing to do that so Kellie wouldn't have to? Would he be able to let her? She was sexy and loved it when she teased him, though he knew it was done in jest. This was no joke and he couldn't stop thinking about it. Would Tracie really keep it a secret? He believed she would, but could he? Would it help their relationship, assuming they got back together, if he wasn't so fixated on getting a blow job all the time?

Unfortunately what he thought had been the major issue has been supplanted by another – his need to be desired. Could Kellie change in this area? He knew she loved him; that was never the issue. Could he express that love as desire? Could she do it the way he needed? The feeling was certainly inside of her, but could she bring it to the surface and let it show? He didn't want to attempt a reconciliation only to have it fail. He couldn't handle that and would probably be even worse for her. He did something he'd been doing for over a week now, he stared at that text. He almost responded several times even going so far as to compose a message, but never sent it. He didn't want to jump back in and be right where they were before. He looked at the text again, then dialed the phone.

"Hello"

"Hi Tracie, it's Chet. Could we get together to chat? My head is spinning and I need someone sane to talk to.

"And no normal people were available so you called me?"

He laughed. "You're a hell of a lot saner than most people I know."

"That's sad. I have to head out for a bit, is eight tonight okay?"

"Perfect. Meet at the bar?"

"I'd rather not tonight. Got beer at home?"

"No, but I'll go get some."

"Good, I'll stop by about eight or so."

"See you then."

Chet straightened up the house and took a quick inventory of the refrigerator. He went out to the convenience store and picked up beer, chips and dip. He was at the register paying when a voice called to him.

"Chet?"

He turned to the sound. "Oh, hi Bob. How's it going?"

"I'm fine," Bob said. "How about *you*?

Where've you been?"

"Been keeping to myself lately."

"I'll say, how about a quick beer?"

"I don't think so."

"Come on, just one. I'll even buy."

They went to a bar near his house. Bob was one of the friends he'd been avoiding since the split. All his buddies thought he was nuts and he didn't want to explain the breakup *ad naseum*. He knew he couldn't avoid his friends forever, nor did he really want to. He just didn't want to be with them right now.

Bob held up his beer in toast. "It's about time."

"I know," Chet said. "It's just –"

"Hey, no need to explain. Let's just say I'm here for you and leave it at that. Deal?"

"Deal." They clinked glasses.

They chatted about sports and their jobs, had a second beer and then a third. Chet was finally starting to relax. He checked his watch, plenty of time before Tracie came over. Talk turned to Bob's wife, Claudia and the kids. Chet thought for a moment, hesitating to ask what was on his mind.

Chet sipped his beer. "You've been married a while now, let me ask you – is sex still the same?"

Bob laughed. "Sure, it's the same sex...over and over again. It never changes."

"You know what I mean. Is it the same as it was in the beginning?"

"Of course not. That excitement wears off and you settle into a routine, hey I'm forty-six now. In the beginning you live for sex, now it's just part of your daily life...though it's not exactly daily...more like monthly."

"Funny," Chet said.

"Look Chet, we know each other for over ten years, I know you. What are you really asking?"

Chet downed the rest of his beer and signaled for another. He thought about it for a moment and wasn't going to ask but the alcohol loosened his tongue.

"Does Claudia still suck you off?"

Bob laughed. "Not so much. Back in the day she could suck the chrome off a trailer hitch and she loved doing it. That stopped years ago. Now I get a blow job on my birthday and I better not cum in her mouth."

"Doesn't it bother you?"

"It did for a while but other things are more important. She's a good woman, a good mother and she loves me."

"You don't miss it?"

Bob laughed and drank from his beer. "You know the waitress Marge at the *Fife and Drum*? For twenty bucks she'll suck you off in the back room. If I feel the need I go in for a beer and let her take care of me."

"What if Claudia finds out?"

Bob gave his head a little shake. "Funny

thing, one day I really needed it and asked Claudia to blow me. She said, 'what's the matter? Marge off today?' She said like she was joking but she seems to know somehow."

"Wow."

Bob stood up to leave. "Man, that girl loved your sorry ass. If that's the reason you guys broke up....."

He came back home about an hour before Tracie was due to come over. He helped himself to another beer to keep the buzz going and sat there thinking about what Bob said. Was he wrong to expect Kellie to make him feel wanted? Was he being too selfish or too needy? Was he throwing away his one chance at love? The more he thought about the more certain he was that the answer was "all of the above." He knew he wanted Kellie back, he missed her so much, but it had to be done the right way and for the right reasons.

He hoped Tracie could help, though he wasn't sure what he was really expecting from her. Did he want her to intervene? He had some things he wanted to ask her about Kellie, but how could he delicately ask her what he really wanted to know – if she was serious about her offer? If so, would he actually let her do it? Would it really help their relationship or doom it? After thinking about what to say he decided to let things take its course and not try to script everything. *Que sera, sera!*

Chapter Twenty-Two

Tracie hung up the phone. She was happy Kellie asked her for the therapist's number, now she hoped she would really call for an appointment. She was worried about her sister, afraid she was losing it. While meeting with a sex therapist may not solve everything, or even anything, it was a step in the right direction. Now it was almost time to meet with Chet. Somehow she wound up in the exact position she had no desire to be in – right between him and Kellie.

Her hair was in a ponytail, she kept the makeup light and she wore her favorite sundress. It was bright, light and showed a lot of cleavage and could wear it without underwear. She thought of it as a "fuck dress" because she didn't have to take it off to have sex, which is what she planned to do after she met with Chet. She was ready to go and still had thirty minutes before she had to leave so she grabbed her favorite toy and vibrated herself to a quick orgasm.

She arrived at Chet's five minutes early and he met her at the door with a beer in hand. She kissed him on the cheek, accepted the beer and made her way to the sofa. He excused himself, went to the kitchen and returned with some chips and salsa and a Sam Adams for himself. They chatted a bit and Tracie could tell he'd been drinking as his movements were just a bit off and his eyes looked a little droopy.

Tracie took a large gulp of her beer. "Looks like I have to catch up, started without me I see."

"Had a couple this afternoon with an old buddy."

She finished her beer and went to the kitchen to help herself to another. She felt his eyes following her and realized she should have worn something a little less revealing. She caught her reflection in the window pane and realized her boobs were practically spilling out of the dress. She chuckled and figured he'd just have to deal with it. She went back to the living room and sat down next to him on the sofa and turned toward him, lifting her knees onto the couch. His eyes went to her cleavage so she waited silently until he looked up. When he did she smiled and watched his face turn beet-red.

"So what did you want to talk about?" Tracie asked.

"I've been doing a lot of thinking and meeting my friend this afternoon pretty much solidified everything for me. I've come to the conclusion that I'm a fucking asshole."

She raised her bottle in a mock cheer.

"Consider yourself lucky. All guys are assholes only most never figure that out."

"Like women are perfect?"

She laughed. "Of course not, women are stupid bitches. Truth about men and women is we're all human."

Chet started talking in circles without ever getting to the point. She let go on him figuring he'd get around to it eventually. He got up for another beer and brought one for her. She drank the first two pretty fast and was starting to feel it. She took a big gulp from the new one anyway as Chet started talking again.

"Thing is Kellie is better than I deserve and I'm such a shit for hurting her like I did."

"So tell her that."

"I will...when the time is right."

"And when will that be?"

"I have no fucking idea. I'm just afraid of getting to that same place where I'm not satisfied again. I have to learn how to accept that she is the way she is."

"I wouldn't wait too long."

"What...what do you mean?"

Tracie ignored him and loaded some salsa on a chip and wolfed it down and chased it with another slug of beer, almost finishing it. She was feeling the buzz now; she got up for another one anyway. There was a bottle of Jack Daniels on the counter so she grabbed that as well along with a couple of glasses. Chet's eyed the bottle down on the coffee table but didn't object when she poured him a shot.

"About her wanting you," Tracie said, "She may never be able to express it the way you want, but she feels it."

"That's why I'm having such a hard time."

She poured two more shots and handed one to Chet. She was well on her way to getting hammered and didn't care. She shifted on the sofa to angle herself toward Chet again. She lifted one leg, bent at the knee, onto the couch and hiked her dress up to make herself comfortable. The move exposed part of her thigh and Chet's eyes were immediately drawn to it. The booze was making her feel flirtatious so she parted her legs just a little. It wasn't quite enough for him to really see anything but provided the illusion that he might. It was just the balance she was looking for. Her eyes wandered to his crotch where she saw a tell-tale bulge and smiled.

He pointed at the bottle but she declined another shot. One more and she'd wind up naked. She fully intended for that to happen later, but not with Chet. She decided it was time to go so she slid her feet to the floor and slipped on her sandals. Chet leaned toward her and she could tell he wanted to ask her something so she paused and looked at him.

"Last time," he began. "Last time we met...you, um...you said you would do something if

Kellie wouldn't."

She wanted to burst out laughing but held her tongue and looked at him as if she had no idea what he was talking about.

"And?" she asked.

"I wanted to know if you were serious."

She gave him a sly smile. She dropped to her knees and moved over in front of him. She unzipped his pants and took out his rock-hard, and very large she was happy to see, cock. She put it in her mouth and took in the entire length in a slow, deep-throating action. He moaned as she came up slowly letting her tongue work the shaft. She thought he might cum right there. She let it slip out of her mouth and slowly stood up leaving him slack-jawed.

"I'm serious. That's just a taste, I'll suck every drop of cum out of you and swallow every bit of it. But only if you guys get back together. By the way, that's a hell of a nice cock."

She went to the door and turned around. He was still sitting on the couch, dick in hand. His eyes were glued to her as she slowly raised her skirt exposing her pussy. His eyes were riveted on her crotch.

"I'm growing a Mohawk, what do you think?"

"Very..very nice."

She laughed, still holding her skirt up. "Go ahead, jerk off – I'll wait."

Chet started beating his cock furiously. She held her skirt up with one hand and used the other to pop one of her boobs free. When she squeezed her nipple his cock exploded in a torrent of semen. When he stopped stroking she quickly fixed her dress, blew him a kiss and left.

She skipped toward her car laughing hysterically. She started the engine and waited a moment to calm down. Before driving away she found her phone, dialed and waited for an answer.

"Will? You alone? Good. Get naked, I'm coming over and I need to pound the living shit out of me!"

Chapter Twenty-Three

The surroundings oozed comfort and warmth, yet Kellie shivered with anxiety. She was sure this would prove to be a fruitless endeavor but there was nothing to lose at this point. So she sat there waiting, her eyes ran over the Monet reproductions on the waiting room walls, a *People Magazine* was open in her hands though she scanned the contents without any of it registering in her brain. She tossed the magazine aside, crossed her arms and legs, leaned back in the chair and closed her eyes. She knew nothing about the woman she was about to see other than what Tracie had told her – she was a really cool lady and if she couldn't help her it was time to join a nunnery. *Sister Kellie of the order no-blow-jobus.*

She just started to doze a bit when the opening of a door startled her. Her eyes blinked open and saw a middle-aged woman with short, iron-grey hair wearing a green pantsuit standing in the doorway smiling at her.

"Kellie? I'm Glenda Plotke, sorry to keep you waiting, come on in."

Kellie rose and walked into Dr. Plotke's office and went toward one of the two chairs situated in front of the classic-style oak desk.

"No, sit over here."

Kellie turned and walked to the side of the office where two low-back armchairs position at a 45° angle to each other were waiting. She picked one and sat down. *At least there's no shrink's couch.* She licked her lips, her mouth suddenly parched. The doctor settled in across from her and stared at her. With no notepad or recording device visible, Kellie wondered how she would remember everything. She fidgeted in her chair and waited but the doctor said nothing, she just smiled at her.

Finally she spoke. "I read your questionnaire but you left much of it blank."

Kellie sat straighter. "Well, Doctor Plotke –"

"Call me Glenda. I'm not a medical doctor, I have a Ph.D. in psychology, thus the 'doctor' but I prefer not to use it."

"Okay...Glenda. I wasn't sure how to answer the questions and some of them were...they were embarrassing."

Glenda shifted. "Stand up please."

Kellie hesitated for a moment, then she stood up. Glenda just stared at her making her uncomfortable.

"Turn around slowly."

She did as instructed until she was facing the woman again.

"You can sit down. How did you feel just now?"

"I...I don't know."

"I think you do. Uncomfortable perhaps?"

Kellie lowered her eyes. "Yes."

"That's the point. For me to help at all you need to be prepared to be uncomfortable – very uncomfortable. Understood?"

"Yes ma'am."

"From what you did write down there seem to be a couple of things you have issues with, why don't you tell me about them?"

Kellie swallowed hard. "It's...it's just like I said in the – "

"I want to hear it in your words."

"Okay," Kellie said. "I can't...I can't perform oral sex."

"You don't suck cock."

Kellie's eyes opened wide but Glenda just let out a little laugh.

"Let's talk about language," Glenda said. "If you use uptight or 'proper' language you'll never relax. Call a blow job a blow job."

"I'm sorry, I just didn't want to offend you."

Glenda laughed louder. "I'm a sex therapist for god's sake. I may be quite a bit older than you but I've heard it all, seen it all and you can be damn well sure I've done it all. There is nothing you can say that will surprise me or shock me, and you damn well won't offend me. So tell me, have you *ever* had a cock in your mouth?"

Kellie felt her face flush and she just nodded affirmatively.

"Good," Glenda said. "Tell me about it and take your time. I want every little detail."

Kellie told her the entire story of what Travis did to her and how it affected her relationships with every guy she was ever with. Glenda listened patiently, asking occasional questions for clarification but otherwise just letting Kellie tell her story. She felt a sense of relief when she finished.

"That's quite a story," Glenda said. "That would certainly be a traumatic experience for anyone. Since that time have you ever felt a desire to suck a cock?"

She shook her head. "The thought of it repulses me. Even with Chet, my ex, I tried to lick it and kiss it but even that made me retch."

"But he must've understood somewhat, I mean you were engaged."

A tear rolled down Kellie's cheek. "He was okay with it for a while – until he wasn't."

"So he left because you wouldn't blow him."

"That's what I thought," Kellie said. "Turns out there *was* something else."

"Which was?"

"He said..." Kellie started to sob. "He said he didn't feel like I wanted him...that's bullshit."

"He told you this?"

"No, he told my sister Tracie. He...he told her

I never made him feel like I wanted him sexually. I can't help it, I'm not wired that way...I'm not a slut."

Glenda stood up and went to her desk, coming back a moment later with a box of tissues. Kellie thanked her, wiped her eyes and tried to compose herself. She took a deep breath and waited for Glenda to continue.

"Let's shift gears for a moment," Glenda said. "Do you have orgasms?"

Kellie dabbed at her eyes. "Yes, I mean not the earth-shaking ones they talk about in *Cosmopolitan*, but I have them."

"Do yourself as favor, don't get sex advice from Cosmo! Now tell me, when was the last time you had an orgasm? I mean a good one."

Kellie thought about it a moment and the answer surprised her. She had totally put it out of her mind until now. Not only was it a recent orgasm but it was an extremely rare "big one," and what she was fantasizing about shocked her. Unlike most of her recent masturbation, she wasn't thinking about Chet.

"It was last week," Kellie said, "last Tuesday."

"Not so long ago," Glenda said. "Was it from masturbation?"

Kellie nodded.

"How often do you play with yourself?"

"Once every week or two, rarely more often than that. Usually when I can't sleep; it helps me relax."

"Was this one of those times?" Glenda asked.

"No, this was different. I was, I...I was *horny*."

"I see. Tell me about it and take your time. What led up to it, what were you thinking about, how did you do it and how did you feel afterward?"

Kellie wasn't sure how to begin as she was still trying to wrap her head around her realization. She did get horny once in a while, usually with the aid of alcohol, but there was no booze involved this time. Still it was what she was thinking about that shocked her. Glenda waited silently as she tried to sort everything out in her head. Kellie felt a surprising tingle between her legs as she closed her eyes and recalled the details.

She glanced out the window and saw Jason, he must have forgotten something. She opened the door.

"Hi Jason. Come on in."

Jason hesitated a moment, then stepped inside. She closed the door and turned to face him.

"I...I forgot to give you these back." He held out her keys.

She reached for them and as she was taking them they slipped from her hand. She bent down to pick them up fumbling for a moment before grabbing them. As she started back up her robe billowed open fully exposing her right breast. She quickly covered herself but Jason had been staring right at her and she realized she had just given him another eyeful, nipple and all. His crimson complexion told her all she needed to know.

He started for the door. "I should go."

She reached out and gently touched his shoulder to stop him. He looked up at her as she let the robe slip from her shoulder and fall to the floor. His mouth agape, he stared at her naked breasts as her nipples hardened. She reached for his hands, taking them in hers, and brought them to her chest. He hesitated, then touched her boobs gently.

"Don't they feel nice and soft?"

"Ye...yes."

"Ummm, that feels good, you can suck on them."

Jason lowered his head to her left nipple and sucked softly, then switched to the right and licked and sucked as she ran her fingers through his hair and pulled him in closer. Her back leaned against the closed door as she moaned softly. After a few minutes she pushed him away, took his hand and led him into her bedroom. She reached the side of the bed, turned and kissed him. His lips parted and she explored his mouth with her tongue and allowed him to do so to her. She broke the kiss and pulled his shirt over his head and tossed it aside. She started unfastening his belt and allowed him to finish and slip out of his jeans.

She dropped down onto the bed wearing only her panties and stretched her arms out inviting him to come to her. He lay next to her and resumed kissing, working his way from her mouth, to her neck and down to her boobs. After he sucked on them for a few minutes she nudged him lower, he took the hint and slowly worked his way down kissing her stomach until he reached her panties. She arched her back and lifted her ass up so he could slip them off. As he did so he stared at her bush.

She laughed. "It's pubic hair, *real* women have it. Don't worry, it doesn't bite."

Jason continued slipping the panties off and tossed them aside. He stared at her pussy as his fingers explored her labia and her clit before slipping them inside her. She was soaking wet. She let out a small gasp and felt like she was ready to cum. Jason seemed unsure of what to do so he nudged his head toward her crotch. He positioned himself between her legs and brought his mouth to her vagina. He kissed it and gave it a few tentative licks. She moaned and it seemed to give him confidence and he licked with more enthusiasm.

She pulled his head in closer. "Oh god, that's it...oh yeah. Now fuck me!"

He sat up on his knees looking down at her. "I've...I've never done –"

"It's okay, you're doing great – *now fuck me damn it!*"

Jason supported himself with one hand while the other guided his cock into her. He started thrusting, picking up speed as he gained confidence. She'd already experienced a couple of small orgasms and felt a big one brewing.

"Oh god! Faster, harder....fuck...me...
...harder...yeah...that's it....oh god.......ugh.....oh...oh
yeah!" *ARGHHH!*

Kellie's eyes blinked open as she
remembered where she was. Glenda was looking at
her and smiling. She could feel that her panties were
soaked.

"I'm sorry, I guess I got lost there," Kellie
said.

"I could tell, your nipples were erect the
whole time you were telling me the story."

Kellie hesitated before speaking. "Am...am I
some kind of pedophile?"

Glenda shook her head and laughed. "God
no. You said he was seventeen, right?"

"Yes, he's seventeen."

"That's old enough to consent. You're no
pedophile, you're a woman who enjoyed a very
healthy sexual fantasy."

"That's a relief."

"Let me ask you this, what did you do to
him?"

"What do you mean?"

"You described, in great detail I might add,
what he did to you. What did you do to him?
Anything?"

"I guess not, I fantasized about him doing
me."

"What was his cock like? Did you fantasize about it?"

"No, no I didn't. I never thought about his cock, just him fucking me with it. Of course, I was fucking myself with my vibrator imagining it was him."

Glenda was jotting down some notes on a pad that seemed to materialize from out of nowhere as Kellie mulled over what it all meant. Jason was a cute kid but she wasn't at all attracted to him, or any other young guy. She wasn't attracted to anyone at all except Chet. Why did she have such an explosive orgasm? Glenda was finishing her notes and putting her pad aside.

"Why him?" Kellie asked. "Why not Chet? You'd think I'd be fantasizing about him."

"You tell me, why him?"

Kellie though about it for a moment. "I don't know. Maybe because I caught him checking out my boob one day, or I accidently flashed him a couple of times."

"Are you sure it was accident?"

"Of course...what do you mean?"

Glenda paused for a moment. "Well, the first time may have been, but is it possible the other times weren't? Perhaps subconsciously you liked the attention."

"But he's just a kid."

"Yet you had one powerful fantasy. When was the last time you had one like that?"

Kellie thought about it. "I don't think I ever did. Am I some kind of sicko?"

"No, as I said before you're a normal woman who had a healthy sexual fantasy. Let me ask you this, if you had to choose just one word to describe Jason what would it be?"

Kellie pondered a moment. "Innocent."

"Innocent – like you were."

Chapter Twenty-Four

Steve spent the week out of the office more than in. As such he only saw Kellie in passing a few times. He wanted to get her sister's phone number but didn't know how to ask her without it seeming awkward. He could have messaged Tracie through Facebook but he was an old-fashioned kind of guy and wanted to call her. He was hoping to take her out on the weekend but tomorrow was Friday so he would have to ask Kellie as delicately as possible for the number, that is if he actually saw Kellie.

He walked into the office Thursday afternoon after spending most of the day in the field. He went to the reception desk to pick up his messages and found a large stack. Leslie was across the room making copies.

"Is Kellie in?" he asked.

Leslie looked up from the copy machine. "She had some sort of appointment to go to so she cut out early."

"No worries, I'll catch her tomorrow."

"She's taking tomorrow off," Leslie said. "Why don't you call her cell, she just left."

"Good idea, you have the number?"

Leslie started moving away from the copier, then stopped. "There's a list in my desk drawer, right on top."

Steve opened the draw and removed a laminated sheet with cell phone numbers for the office staff. She found Kellie and saw that right under her number was another that said "Emergency Contact" and listed Tracie's name and number. He jotted both numbers down and put the card back in the drawer.

"Got it, thanks Leslie."

A smile lit up his face as he walked to his office. By the time he got there he realized he had an erection. He sat in the desk chair and let his hand rub his crotch lightly as he tried to decide on the best time to call. His fingers moved from rubbing his cock through his pants to the computer keyboard. He logged onto *Facebook* and navigated his way to Tracie's profile. Her read through her timeline and the "about me" section again. He tried accessing her page on *Fetlife* but the office computer system would not allow access since it blocked sites with adult content. He made up his mind to call her later that night. His cock had other ideas so he used his cell phone to dial her number.

"Hello"

"Tracie, it's Steve – Kellie's friend, we met at the bar."

"Steve?...oh hi! What's up?"

Steve swallowed hard and beads of perspiration formed on his forehead. "I...I was wondering if you mike like to grab a bite Saturday night....if you're not busy."

"Oh, I can't Saturday."

The air went out of Steve's lungs and his mood instantly darkened. As nervous as he was he hadn't considered that she would turn him down.

"I see, no worries then."

"How about tomorrow?" Tracie asked.

Steve's heart started beating again. "Tomorrow would be fantastic. Do you like French food? I was thinking Andrè's at the Ritz Carlton."

"Oh wow, I've always wanted to go there. Should I meet you there?"

"We can meet at the hotel bar, say seven?"

"Seven? Sure, that works. Oh wow, I'm so excited!"

"Okay, I'll see you tomorrow at seven."

Steve ended the call. He realized he had pacing back and forth across his office during the call. He also became aware of a raging hard-on. He took two quick steps toward the door and locked it. He unzipped his pants, took out his cock and started stroking while he walked back to his desk and found a napkin. As he was about to cum he brought it up to the head but he ejaculated with such force that a large stream shot across his desk and landed on the papers spread out across the top.

Chapter Twenty-Five

Tracie hung up the phone and screamed. A guy's call just didn't normally excite her like this. She went to her bedroom closet and looked at her wardrobe; there was nothing suitable for a high-class place like Andrè's. She had a nice dress she'd worn to a friend's wedding but that wasn't quite what she was looking for. She would have to go shopping. Now she wished she had made the date for Saturday so she'd have more time.

She went to the bathroom and looked at herself in the mirror, definitely time to get a haircut too. She dropped her jeans down to mid-thigh and lowered her panties. She ran her fingers through her pubes and contemplated shaving them again. She looked in the mirror and decided the hair had grown in enough so it could stay; she was done with the "bald look" for good. She pulled her pants back up and went to the kitchen for a soda. She looked at the clock and figured she could catch Kellie before she left work. She dialed her sister's cell phone.

"Hello"

"Hey sis...are you driving? I thought you'd still be at work."

"On my way to get the pearly-whites cleaned."

"Oh what joy!" Tracie said. "Did you see Glenda? I figured you would call me, how did it go?"

"Oh fine. We found out I'm nuts."

"Funny."

"Seriously, I'm looney-tunes, bat-shit crazy. The good news is I'm not a pedophile, though even that was touch-and-go for a while."

"Okay, so what's the official diagnosis? Are you asexual?"

"No, she doesn't think so. She says I have a repressed sexuality and whenever my sexuality does come to the surface I push it back down, I also have 'oral anxiety' because of what happened to me."

Tracie bit her lip. "I'd like to cut that bastard's balls off. Can she help you?"

"She's going to try. I have to allow myself to enjoy sex instead of treating it like an obligation. "

Tracie shook her head and smiled. "Sounds like something a certain sister has been telling you for years."

"Yeah, yeah, stop gloating. There's more – I have to go to cock class tomorrow."

"Cock class?"

"Dick school, Penis 101, a Pecker Primer. It's a sex education class. If I learn about the workings of the male anatomy maybe I won't fear it so much. I'm already working on my introduction: Hi, my name is Kellie and I'm a cock-a-phobe."

Tracie laughed. "You are in much better spirits."

"It's the relief from finding out I'm not a pedophile."

"Why would you think you were pedophile?" Tracie asked.

"I'll tell you about it when I see you, it's a long story."

Tracie was happy to hear her sister in such a good mood. She hoped identifying the problem would actually lead to a solution. At the very least she might be able to find away to deal with her issue and accept it.

"What time is your class?" Tracie asked.

"Ten in the morning but I'm taking the whole day off."

"Good, that means you can come shopping with me."

"Not for more of your toys I hope."

Tracie smiled. "No, I need to buy a killer dress."

"What's the occasion?"

"Steve's taking me to Andrè's."

"Andrè's? Do you know how expensive that place is? He's taking *you* there?"

"Hey princess, you had your chance. You didn't want him, remember?"

"I suppose you're going to spank him for desert."

Tracie giggled like a schoolgirl. "After dinner at that place he can spank *me*! Though, I do have to thank you for giving him my number."

"I didn't give him your number."

"Really?"

Chapter Twenty-Six

The class was being held in a generic-looking office park. Kellie located building and Suite 7G, there was no indication of the type of business. The sign simply said SA Seminars, though she now knew that SA stood for Sexual Awareness. She found a parking space and walked toward the door, pausing for a deep breath before she opened it. She walked in to a reception area with a large desk and few empty chairs. An older, casually dressed woman walked in and asked her name. She was immediately led to a conference room with an oval table with four chairs on each side and another at each end.

Four women were seated around the table and the each looked directly at her as she walked in, obviously sizing her up. She wondered why each of them was here and she assumed they were thinking the same about her. There was a heavyset girl in her early twenties, an older woman in her fifties with the other two being somewhere in the vicinity of her age. She muttered a greeting and sat next to the older lady. Just as she settled in another woman walked in and made her way to the front of the room.

The woman was attractive, forty-something and exuded confidence. She pushed a button and a screen lowered from the ceiling. She passed out a booklet and pushed another button and a projector started warming up, its light becoming visible on the screen.

"Hi everyone, my name is Amanda; I'll be your instructor this morning. We're going to start with a short video."

The video began with an introduction to the company and its history. Then it introduced the class – *Male Sexual Anatomy* – and played the kind of animated video one might see in junior high. Kellie started watching the clock on the wall and wondered if it would be impolite to leave early. Though she hadn't been sure exactly what to expect, this certainly wasn't it. Mercifully the video ended after about ten minutes.

"Now that we have that out of the way," Amanda said, "we can get down to business. Each of you has been referred here because you have something in common. You have some sort of anxiety or issue with the male anatomy, or as we refer to it in this class by its highly technical name – the dick."

The last comment elicited a round of laughter and the tension seemed to drain out of the room. Amanda opened a cabinet and withdrew five boxes and handed them out. Kellie opened it to find an anatomically correct rubber penis. The other women were laughing as they took theirs out of the box. The balls had a flat bottom so it would stand up on the tabletop.

"Okay," Amanda said. "You all have your dicks. What do you notice about them?"

"There small," Cecilia, the chubby girl said. "I have a much bigger dildo at home."

Amanda laughed. "They aren't meant to be dildos. These are actually bigger than the average penis. The ones you have are six inches long, the average man is slightly more than five and a half inches erect."

"Then why does every guy claim to have seven or eight?" asked Janice, the older woman.

"Yeah," said Lisa, one of the thirtyish girls, "guys can do precision carpentry down to the millimeter but can't measure their own cock."

"It's ego," Amanda said. "Guys obsess about how big they are – or aren't."

Amanda reviewed the different parts of the penis using the dildos as a reference. She explained the purpose function of each part. Kellie paid much greater attention when she started talking about oral sex and the techniques used. After explaining that their rubber dicks were all new and sterile she had them practice sucking on them. She had no problem with this part since the dick wasn't alive and it wasn't much different than when she practiced sucking on a cucumber.

While she and her classmates were doing the exercise Amanda was arranging chairs in a semicircle at the front of the room. When she was done she got everyone's attention and asked them to choose a seat and sit down. When everyone was in their place she explained it was time for the next portion of the class. Amanda looked toward the door and nodded. A good looking guy in his mid-twenties walked into the room wearing a bathrobe. Kellie noticed Cecilia biting her lower lips as her now-erect nipples showed themselves through her shirt. The guy made his way to the front of the room and stood before them.

Amanda smiled. "It's now time for a live demonstration. Timothy, if you please?"

Timothy opened his robe and tossed it aside. He wasn't an Adonis, but he was in good shape. His pubic hair was shaved; his cock was flaccid and seemed to be similar in size to their dildos. The younger girls were giggling while Janice seemed to be embarrassed. Kellie just tried to look at it without a feeling of revulsion. Okay so far. Timothy stood with his hands on his hip as his penis began to grow until it was fully erect. Amanda walked over to him with a tape measure, the soft kind a tailor would use. She put one end at the point where the penis met the pubic bone and other to the midpoint of the head.

Amanda held up the tape. "Seven and a

quarter inches. That's the proper way to measure the length."

"My boyfriend says he's seven inches and he's nowhere near that big," Lisa said. "He probably measures from the asshole out!"

There was laughter all around but all eyes were fixed on Timothy's cock. Amanda assured each of them that their model had been recently tested and was disease free. Then she instructed them to feel his cock with their finger tips and notice the difference in the softness and texture between the head and the shaft. They each did so.

"Now the next part is optional," Amanda said. "You can take it in your mouth and see how it feels and tastes but remember – you're not giving a blowjob."

Cecilia wasted no time and was on her knees in front of him, her mouth all over his cock.

Chapter Twenty-Seven

Tracie sat in the stylist's chair and looked in the mirror as she turned her head from side to side. Her hair hadn't been this short since high school. The tint lightened the color just enough to give it the highlights she wanted. She decided she liked it, the style said sophisticated and *mature*. She was thirty-one and it was about time she grew up. She glanced at her newly-manicured nails with the white polish and French tips; she'd even had her eyebrows waxed. Yes, she definitely liked the look and she hoped Steve would as well.

Next she went to the mall. She had some time before Kellie would meet her there so she went to the food court for some coffee. Cup in hand she browsed the storefronts looking at dresses on the mannequins on display. Nothing caught her eye so she kept strolling. She came to the lingerie shop and looked at the mannequin dressed as a dominatrix and laughed – *amateur*! She finished her coffee, tossed the cup in the trashcan and went inside. If she was doing an entire makeover including a dress she figured new undies were in order as well. She was looking at the panties when her cell phone chirped with a text from Kellie. She replied with her location and resumed browsing. She selected a couple of bottoms and started looking at the matching bras.

A saleswoman a little older than she was came over. "Hi, I'm Marcie. Can I help you select something?"

"I was looking for the matching bra."

Marcie looked her up and down. "You look to be about a forty double D, is that right?"

Tracie shook her head in amazement. "Bull's-eye."

Marcie took the panties from her hand and put them back where they came from. "Come with me."

Tracie followed the saleswoman to a table toward the back of the store. It was apparently the well-endowed woman's section. Marcie picked up a similar pair of panties to the ones she had been holding and handed them to her.

"You don't want to be mismatched," Marcie said. "Now what look are you going for? The 'let them have a little peek and want more' look or the 'leave them drooling on the floor curled up in the fetal position' look?"

Tracie let out a very loud laugh. "Let's have him drooling like a baby."

"What's so funny?" Kellie asked as she walked up. "My god, I *love* your hair!"

"Thanks. My friend Marcie here is helping me with my body armor."

"Well you can lock and load those boobs in the fitting room," Marcie said. "Try them on and see how they look."

Tracie took the underwear and quickly tried them on. The fit was perfect and she loved the look. White lace with her large nipples just peaking out the top of the bra, the bottoms showed her burgeoning black triangle perfectly. *That is so sexy, I was nuts to ever shave.* She changed back into her own underwear and went to the register to pay. She had never spent so much for a bra and panties before but she felt it was worth every penny. You can't put a price on sexy.

Tracie found Kellie browsing at a table. "Still shopping in the prude section?"

"Hey, at least I'm comfortable."

"Sexy is as sexy does," Tracie said. "You can't be sexy if you don't feel sexy. Come with me."

Tracie took her by the hand and led her across the store to where Marcie was arranging a table of panties.

"Marcie, this is my sister Kellie. Set her up with something really hot."

Marcie eyed Kellie's figure. "Thirty-four B?"

"That's right," Kellie said. "But I really don't—"

"Right this way," Marcie said.

Tracie watched with amusement. Despite her protests, Kellie was getting into it. Marcie helped her select a couple of sets and she took them into the fitting room. She came out a few minutes later and came over to her and put the underwear down on a nearby table.

"You didn't like them?" Tracie asked.

"No, I did, they're really nice. But did you see the price of this stuff?"

Tracie shook her head and picked the lingerie off the table and walked toward the register. Kellie followed behind her trying to take it away but Tracie refused to let her have them.

"It's on me," Tracie said.

"I can't let you do that."

"I'm doing it. Like I said, you can't be sexy if you don't feel sexy, consider it part of your therapy. Now what's this pedophile crap?"

Sitting in the food court Tracie listened as her sister explained the pedophilia comment as they each ate a salad. Kellie also told her about the class that morning. She laughed at the part about the life-size dildos but was truly surprised about the live demonstration. If she'd known about that she might've gone herself.

"So these women were all over that guy's dick?" Tracie asked.

"Yeah, even the older lady couldn't get it in her mouth fast enough. You should have seen the poor guy suffer."

Tracie laughed. "What about you? Did you even try?"

Kellie shook her head. "I couldn't. But hey, I watched without puking up breakfast. That's progress at least."

Chapter Twenty-Eight

Kellie wasn't just paying an empty compliment; she really loved her sister's new hairstyle. She kept glancing at it as they walked through the mall and glanced at Tracie's reflection in the storefront's glass whenever they stopped to look at a display. She looked like a totally different person. Her sister seemed sophisticated rather than trashy, and though she never thought of her in those terms she had to admit that was the vibe she sometimes gave off. The old style may have suited Tracie's kinky lifestyle but the new one was more fitting of the way she like to think of her sister.

Tracie stopped in front of the most upscale clothing store in the mall and paused a moment before walking inside. Kellie followed her in. She was holding the bags from both of their purchases from the lingerie shop. Though she had protested, she was happy her sister insisted on buying it for her. It did make her feel sexy even if she had no one to wear it for, though Tracie had snidely suggested she could wear them the next time she flashed Jason. The funny thing was the thought of that excited her. *Bat-shit crazy!*

Tracie stopped in front of a rack of evening gowns. Kellie looked at the display mannequin on top of the rack and had to agree the dress was gorgeous. As her sister searched for her size Kellie looked at the tag and blanched.

"Did you look at the price?"

"No," Tracie said. "I don't care, it's about time I treated myself. Besides, he's taking me to Andrè's and I'm feeling the need to be girlie."

"As opposed to slutty?"

"Very funny."

Tracie selected a dress off the rack and made her way to the fitting room. Kellie followed her in and sat on a bench as her sister went into a booth. She came out a few minutes later and Kellie was absolutely floored. The dress was a perfect fit. It was teal green which suited her skin color perfectly and accentuated her figure while minimizing the flaws, though most guys would never get past the boobs which were on full display.

"You are fucking gorgeous," Kellie said.

"I love it. I'm getting it, let's go."

They wound up back at the food court, this time for smoothies. Kellie couldn't imagine dropping so much money on a dress but she had to admit her sister would certainly fit in at Andrè's. Kellie searched for a word to describe this new version of her sister and decided on *classy*.

"I still can't get over the new look," Kellie said. "What inspired such a big change? It can't be just a date."

"No, but that was the catalyst. It's been a long time since a regular guy asked me on a real date. I just decided it's time to grow up."

"Do you even remember how to go on a real date? I mean it wouldn't be proper to start spanking him in the middle of the restaurant."

"Funny," Tracie said. "The weird thing is that I haven't even thought about him that way. I almost feel *normal*."

Kellie laughed. "That's hard to believe. What if he finds out about your, um, perversions?"

"If we hit it off I'll tell him. If it's just one date then no harm, no foul and we each go our merry way."

"Something tells me you'll hit it off."

Tracie looked her in the eye. "I hope so....I really hope so."

Kellie drove back home from the mall, arriving two hours earlier than normal after her adventurous day off. She brought her packages in with her, one with the lingerie and the other her souvenir dick from that morning's cock class. The underwear she put away but the dick stayed upright on her coffee table. She had homework – exercises that Glenda prescribed for her. She started by getting undressed and slipping into her robe.

Glenda wanted her to get in touch with herself, literally. She was to spend a minimum of sixty minutes touching her body all over, but not in a sexual way. She was instructed to start with her earlobes and work her way down to her feet. She was to use her fingers to gently touch each part and concentrate on how it felt. She was to note the texture of her skin and how one part was different than another. Ear lobes were different from lips, which were different from the skin on her body, her nipples, her navel, her pussy, the rougher skin on her knees, the bottom of her feet. Glenda's point is that the entire body, especially the mind, is a sex organ.

Kellie did exactly as ordered and paid attention to every feeling, every touch. When she finished she re-tied her robe and jotted down her response in a notebook. Then she went to the kitchen and poured herself a glass of wine and selected a frozen entrée from the freezer for dinner. She shook her head. *Tracie gets Andrè's and I get Lean Cuisine.*

After she ate she took her wine into the living room and proceeded to do the second part of her homework. Glenda instructed her to get into a relaxed position, close her eyes and meditate. Once she achieved a state of relaxation she was to fantasize. She had explained to her that it was important to think about sex – a lot. She could fantasize about anything as long as it was something out of the ordinary for her and outside of her comfort zone. It should excite her but not be so unusual that it could never happen. The idea was to stretch her boundaries and open her mind to possibilities she may either not have considered or would normally be too timid to try. The more she pushed the envelope the better since it was, after all, a fantasy.

She was back at the mall, only this time with Chet....

Blistering heat raged all day and they came to the mall to wander around and cool off. She was wearing a light sundress, the one he always said was his favorite. He liked it because the skirt was fairly short and barely covered her butt cheeks and the top was loose allowing him to sneak peeks at her breasts as he walked next to her. Though she was not what could be remotely considered well endowed, Chet always said he loved her boobs because they had a perfect shape, great nipples and a nice jiggle to them. They walked hand-in-hand past the storefronts until they reached the food court.

Kellie sat at a table while Chet went to get a couple of smoothies. She watched him as he waited at the counter and realized what a great ass he had. She wanted to grab it and wondered what it would be like to give him a rim job. He never asked her to do it but she was pretty sure he'd like it. She added it to her to-do list. She watched him as he walked back to the table. He handed her the smoothie and sat down next to her. She kicked off a sandal and rubbed the side of his calf with her bare foot as they sat there people watching without saying a word. When she finished her drink she excused herself to use the restroom. She didn't have to pee but she did check her makeup. She also removed her panties and held them in her hand as she went back to the food court. It gave her a thrill to walk out knowing she was naked under her dress.

Chet was watching her as she walked back to the table and held out her empty hand to help him up. He started walking toward the main part of the mall when she tugged him in a different direction. He seemed puzzled but followed her to the far end of the court which was unoccupied. She was pretending to check out a couple of the overhead menus but was really leading him to a raised planter that jutted a few feet out from the wall. She moved behind it pulling him along with her. She turned and faced the center of the court, satisfied that no one could see her, not from the waist down anyway.

"What are you doing?" Chet asked.

"I need you to hold this." She handed him her panties.

He looked wide-eyed at the underwear in his hand as she leaned forward at the waist and flipped her skirt up exposing her bare but. She spread her legs apart a little and supported herself by leaning her forearms on the planter.

"Fuck me."

"Are you crazy? Here?"

"Just fuck me, damn it."

She felt him maneuver behind her as he unzipped his pants. She reached one hand back, found his rock-hard cock and guided her to her soaking wet pussy. She bit her lip to stifle a gasp as he pushed his way in. He started thrusting lightly, obviously trying to be discrete. She started bucking back into him, timing her movement to the rhythm of his thrusts. His breathing became shallow as he started pumping faster. She felt light headed as she felt herself nearing orgasm. He grunted and pulled her to him and held on tight as he came. She let out a small cry as she climaxed along with him. She caught her breath as he pulled back and slipped out of her. She could feel his warm semen as it left her pussy and ran down the inside of her thigh....

Kellie opened her eyes and realized she'd been fucking herself with cock from her class that morning. She slipped it out of her vagina and caught her breath as she recovered. *Whoa, that was a big one.*

Chapter Twenty-Nine

The reflection in the mirror was someone else – it had to be. Tracie was not the type of person who had a problem admitting when she looked good but she had never, ever looked *this* good. The dress, the shoes, her hair, her nails, her makeup, it was all flawless. She told Kellie she didn't look at the price of the dress but of course she had. It cost her almost two weeks pay, and that was gross not net. Looking in the mirror told her it was well worth it, no regrets at all. *Damn!*

Though she typically ran late, this time she was ready to go long before she needed to be. She visualized the evening in her mind and cautioned herself against drinking too much lest she do or say something stupid. Thoughts of potential missteps started running through her head. She realized what she was doing and made herself stop. Positive thoughts only, negative thinking invited disaster. Instead she started picturing what would go right. She went to her bedroom and took a good look to make sure it was presentable just in case. Though she would prefer to go to his place she knew he had a son and he probably wouldn't take her to his home. She stopped again realizing she was getting way ahead of herself. The ringing of her phone snapped her train of thought.

"Hello"

"Hi Tracie, it's Cheryl."

"Oh hi."

Tracie had totally forgotten about the scene she'd agreed to participate in. Her policy was never to back out to something you agreed to do but the thought of having sex with Cheryl and Daryl didn't appeal to her at all. In fact none of her usual romps had entered her mind lately.

"We're able to get that doctor's office for Saturday afternoon," Cheryl said. "I was hoping you were ready to play."

"I'm sorry Cheryl, I can't."

"Oh that's too bad, I'll see if I can arrange a different day. What works for you?"

Tracie took a deep breath. "Cheryl, I'm really sorry but I'm not going to be able to do it. I just can't right now."

"I see."

Tracie felt bad especially since Cheryl's disappointment was so obvious. On the other hand she felt an overwhelming sense of relief since she never really wanted to play with them in the first place. She looked at the clock and realized she should have left five minutes ago and hurried out the door.

She still arrived at the Ritz hotel and Andrè's five minutes early and pulled up to the valet. The attendant opened her door and gave her a look when she got out. He probably thought the dress was worth more than her decade-old Honda Accord. She walked to the entrance and a gloved doorman held the door for her and nodded a greeting as she walked inside. There was piano music playing and she could see a small dance floor off to the side of the room. A hostess greeted her but she told her she was meeting someone at the bar. She walked down a wide hallway past the mahogany-paneled walls decorated with expensive-looking oil paintings of English fox hunting scenes and entered the bar area. With her head held high and a smile on her face she felt the eyes on her as every head turned to watch her walk by.

There was a lump in her throat and her heart skipped a beat when she saw him waiting for her at the end of the bar. He was dressed in dark suit, white cotton Oxford shirt with a maroon tie. She saw his broad shoulders and the taper of his waist as he stood to greet her. She knew he looked good and she thought he was really hot when she met him but he was so...so *handsome*. By the look her gave her she knew he was pleased as well. He held out the stool for her as she sat down. As she settled into her seat the bartender placed a drink in front of her.

"I took the liberty of ordering you an apple martini," Steve said. "If you prefer something else..."

"No, this is perfect!"

His eyes didn't leave her. "I thought you looked beautiful when we met, but..."

"I clean up pretty good, huh?" Tracie laughed.

"You are absolutely stunning."

The heat rose in Tracie's cheeks. "Thank you."

Chapter Thirty

The week seemed to move from one crisis to another. Nothing at work was going right, yet Chet didn't care. All he could think about was what Tracie had done – what *he* had done. What he thought would be the perfect solution was anything but. The ridiculous fantasy of having a relationship with Kellie while getting blowjobs from Tracie was just that – ridiculous. Even if Tracie was true to her word and kept it a secret he would never be able to handle the guilt. Everything was so much clearer to him now. If he was to have a life with Kellie it had to be only Kellie and nothing on the side. If he was in he had to be *all in*.

So much of what Bob said to him hit home. Kellie was not perfect but she was perfect for him. She loved him and he knew it. Everything he was so worried about was, in the long run, trivial. He wanted a partner in life, someone he could grow old with. Maybe she wasn't as sexually exciting as Jean and she wasn't adventurous like Tracie, but she had given him so much more they ever could. He was such an idiot and he hoped it wasn't too late.

His biggest problem now was working up the nerve to contact her. Despite what her sister said she may have moved on mentally and might not want him back. He certainly couldn't blame her after the way he ended the relationship. Would contacting her just be rubbing salt in the wound? Would she reject him? The mental gymnastics paralyzed him and kept him from doing what he knew he should.

Every day he stared at the text she'd sent him. Maybe she was drunk liked Tracie said but she still sent it. Sent it at a time she was obviously vulnerable and feeling alone. And he never responded. *I'm such an ass.*

Chapter Thirty-One

The waiter handed a menu to Tracie and then to Steve before silently backing away. The table was discretely tucked into a quiet corner and lit by candlelight. Everything looked so good she had no idea what to order. There was something strange about the menu; it took her a moment to realize what it was.

"There are no prices."

Steve chuckled. "That's the way it's done in traditional style restaurants, only the host has one with prices."

"I assume by 'traditional' you mean expensive?"

He laughed again. "You could say that."

"This is great, but I would have been very happy without you spending so much."

"It's not a problem, really. Besides, I haven't been on a date in so long that I wanted to do it right."

"How long has it been? Is this the first since...since –?"

"Since my wife died? Yes."

"Steve, I'm sorry. Kellie told me what happened."

The waiter came back to take their order. Kellie still hadn't looked at the menu carefully so she suggested that he order for both of them. It would also help her feel less guilty about spending too much. After she assured him that there was nothing on the menu she wouldn't eat, he glanced at the menu again before putting it down.

He looked up at the waiter. "We'll have Oysters Rockefeller for an appetizer and the Caesar salad for two. For our entre we'll have the Chateaubriand. We'll also have a bottle of the Chateau Margaux."

The waiter didn't write anything down. "Very good, sir."

The waiter returned with the bottle of red wine and uncorked it at the table. He poured a small amount into the glass next to Steve for him to sniff and taste. After he indicated that it was good he poured a glass for Tracie after which he filled Steve's glass. They toasted each other and drank a sip.

"Oh my god," Tracie said. "This is delicious."
"I'm glad you like it."

The oysters were served and they sat quietly while they ate them. After the plates were cleared they made small talk until the waiter returned with a cart and prepared the salad tableside while Tracie watched in fascination. The ingredients were mixed and placed into two bowls and set down in front of them.

"That was unreal," Tracie said. "I didn't know all of that stuff went in a Caesar."

"Taste it."

She did. "This is *unbelievable!*"

They ate slowly and when they finished the salad the waiter cleared their plates. He returned a moment later and set down two very tiny spoons and a very small dish with something in it. Tracie picked up the spoon and tasted it and a surprised look appeared on her face.

"This is sherbet, why are they serving desert?"

Steve laughed and covered his mouth. "It's a sorbet, it's meant to cleanse the palate before the main course."

The waiter cleared the plates and returned pushing another cart. He opened the lid to reveal the Chateaubriand which her carved in front of them and place on their plates. He added a side of vegetables and potatoes and refilled their wine glasses before retreating once more. Tracie took a bite of her meat and sighed with delight.

"I could get used to this."

Steve didn't say anything and she suddenly realized he might have taken that the wrong way and her face reddened.

"I didn't mean I expect to be treated like this," she said. "I just meant –"

"Relax, I understand what you mean. I'm glad you're enjoying it. Besides, you *should* be treated like this."

"I'm sorry. I guess I'm feeling a little guilty, I can't imagine how much this is costing."

"Well let's give that a rest," he said. "You'll find out sooner or later. I was a first round pick of the Raiders more years ago than I care to admit. I received a large signing bonus which Cheryl, my wife, insisted we bank and never touch. I also had a four year contract. I blew my knee out in training camp for my second year which made the team decide to cut me. But I did receive an injury settlement for the remainder of the contract which I also banked. Money is not an issue."

"Kellie told me she thought you played football but she didn't know the details. I do see you've stayed in great shape," she said as she blushed again.

Steve shook his head. "Not quite. When my career ended I let myself go and put on quite a few pounds. When Cheryl was diagnosed with cancer I was so angry that I returned to the gym with a vengeance in order to vent so I wouldn't take it out on my family."

"Steve, I'm so –"

"No, it's okay. But let's talk about other things."

They finished dinner but neither one had any room for desert. Instead they moved back to the bar for an after dinner drink. Steve ordered a cognac and Tracie had an Irish coffee. The piano was playing and Steve suggested they dance. Tracie said she wanted to use the restroom first. While in there she fixed her makeup and made sure her hair was still in good shape. She stood back from the mirror to appraise her dress. Satisfied that her new outfit held up well she moved toward the sink and leaned forward. She adjusted her boobs to show maximum cleavage and returned to the bar. He stood up and she took his hand and moved to the dance floor.

He was a much better dancer than she was but he didn't seem to mind. She loved the feel of his hand in hers. She held him close and at one point put her head on his shoulder. She took in the smell of him, the feel of his body, the way his muscles strained against his suit. She lifted her head and looked into his eyes and parted her mouth slightly. He leaned down, brought his lips to hers and gave her a brief, but very tender kiss. Her knees went weak and she could feel that she was extremely wet.

She brought her lips to his ear and whispered, "Would you like to come back to my place?"

He pulled away and smiled at her. "This night has been everything I hoped, if not more. I wouldn't want to ruin the fantasy..."

Her face fell and tears filled her eyes. She wanted to say something but couldn't get the words past the lump in her throat. *He rejected me.*

He smiled at her again and his fingers lifted her chin. "How about we stay here instead? I have a room in the hotel."

Chapter Thirty-Two

Kellie watched an old black and white movie after changing into her pajamas. Of course she had to clean herself up first, and clean the toy dick and put it away. She started thinking that she hadn't been that wet and turned on from masturbating in a very long time but then she realized she'd been just as worked up when she fantasized about Jason the week before. She remembered reading an article in Cosmo that said women reach their sexual peak after age thirty. She was twenty-nine so maybe, just maybe she was finally waking up sexually. *Either that or I'm just bat-shit crazy.*

She looked at the clock and hoped Tracie and Steve were having a good time on their date. Thinking about the restaurant they were at gave her a pang of jealousy for which she quickly admonished herself. Steve was a great guy but she knew it never would have worked between them, a conclusion Steve also came to. She thought he was a nice match for her sister but she couldn't imagine him embracing the lifestyle she led nor could she see Tracie ever settling into a normal relationship.

Hopefully they would have fun for however long it lasted.

She started dozing toward the end of the movie. She heard a buzzing and didn't realize what it was until it happened a second time. She had a text. She glanced at the clock and realized it was after midnight. It was probably just Tracie reporting on her date. She sat up and reached across the table for her phone. She blinked the sleep out of her eyes and hit the button to pull up the message. She did a double-take and fumbled with the phone and dropped it. She picked it up off the floor and read it again as her heart pounded in her chest.

Miss u 2
How r u?

She started tapping out a reply, paused a moment and decided to make him wait a bit. Two minutes later she continued.

Was going to lie and say good, but i m miserable

She waited for what seemed like an eternity. She was tempted to call him but decided not to, if he wants to talk he can call. Finally her phone buzzed.

Ive been a shit and probably have no right to ask, but would you have coffee with me?

She didn't wait to respond this time.

YES

A few more texts allowed them to settle on a time and place. She started thinking about what she would wear as shut off the television and climbed into bed. Naturally she couldn't stop thinking about him. In no time at all her fingers slipped inside her panties.

Chapter Thirty-Three

The door swung open and Tracie stepped inside. Her eyes went wide as she took in the room. It was a mini-suite with a living room area separated by a small partition with the other side consisting of a sleeping area with a king-size bed that had already been turned down. There was a bottle of wine with two glasses set on a small table. Steve removed the cork and let it sit to breathe. She could see he was very nervous so she went up to him and loosened his tie. Using it as a handle, she pulled him down to kiss him. She got a sense of how tall he was when she kicked off her heels, she was tall but he towered at least eight inches over her, if not more.

She helped him out of his suit jacket and hung it over a chair. Then she unfastened his shirt sleeves and then started working on the buttons. As he started taking the shirt off she slipped her hands under his t-shirt and felt his pecs. Lifting the shirt up, she started kissing his chest as he pulled the rest of the way over his head. She turned so he could lower the zipper on her dress and carefully stepped out of it when she did so. In an unsexy moment she walked to the closet to hang it up, she'd spent far too much to risk ruining it. After placing it in the closet she turned to face him and heard an audible gasp and was immediately thankful for the new underwear. *Thank you, Marcie.*

They moved toward each other. His arms went around her as she placed one around his back while the other felt the outline of his enormous cock. Their lips met and she let his tongue into her mouth to probe. They kissed for several minutes until her led her to the bed. She sat down on the edge and wanted to pull him near so as to get her mouth on his cock but he nudged her back onto the bed. He snuggled up next to her and started kissing her forehead and slowly, very slowly moved to her neck. She let out a moan and squirmed as his tongue licked her. He moved down to the top of her boobs, kissed the outside of her bra then went down lower to her belly and kissed her there. He moved lower still.

She thought she was going to pass out when his lips brushed her clit through her panties. He moved to the inside of her thighs and her legs started to quiver as he kissed and licked. He worked his way lower to her knees, then her calves and on to her toes. He gently sucked each one as her fingers gripped the sheets and her back arched. He nudged her and she turned over on her stomach. He started working his way back up. The back of her thighs, her ass, her back, all received attention. When he reached her bra he unfastened it. Finally!

He moved up to her neck and the back of her head, he nudged her and she rolled onto her back again. He kissed her some more. He sat up and slipped her bra off and she felt her boobs slide to her sides.

"My god! They're magnificent!"

She smiled as she slid her hand inside the band of his briefs and felt the tip of his cock. It was sticky with pre-cum and she felt him throbbing as if her were ready to explode. It made her wonder how long it had been for him. She lost her train of thought as his mouth found her left nipple and she pulled her head in and moaned. He hadn't touched her pussy but *she* was ready to cum. While he sucked she was tugging at his underwear and he got the message and slipped them off, though his mouth never left her boob. Her hand wrapped around his cock and she started stroking but his hand stopped her. *He was ready to cum.*

She shifted a little. "Fuck my titties!"

He straddled her as she squeezed her boobs together. As he nestled his cock between her breasts she squeezed them together. He moved back and forth a few times, closed his eyes, grunted and shot a wad of semen that hit her square in the chin. She used her fingers to wipe it off and brought it to her mouth where she greedily licked it up.

"I'm sorry, it's been –"

"I know, it's been a long time. Now you can relax and enjoy yourself. I have feeling there's plenty more where that came from."

"Let me get a towel," he said.

"No. Feed it to me, I want it all."

He used his finger to take the semen from her chest and bring it to her waiting mouth. When he had gotten most of it he started sucking her boobs again. His free hand slid inside her panties and fingered her pussy as she squirmed. He tugged her underwear down and she arched her back to let him slip them off. She smiled when he said "nice" as he eyed her nascent pubes. After he tossed the panties aside she spread her legs wide and he slid down between them. She jumped when his tongue found her clit and she had her first orgasm very soon after. He may have been out of practice but he was incredibly skilled. She had one orgasm after another each one building and more powerful than the one before.

She managed to reach his cock and saw the he was almost hard again. He moved sideways a little so her hand could reach it. She stroked until it was fully erect. He climbed up on his knees and moved between her legs. She let out a loud gasp as he slid inside her. He moved slowly, then fast, then slow again. He varied his motion, paused now and then and kept bring her to the edge. He was bringing himself to another orgasm and as she sensed he was getting close she started bucking and wound up climaxing right along with him.

They held each other close as she rested her head on his chest. She lightly ran her finger over his limp cock and smiled when it started coming back to life after a long rest. When he was about halfway up she wrapped her fingers around the shaft and started jerking him lightly increasing her speed as he grew firmer. When she was sure he wouldn't go back down she climbed on top of him. With his help she guided his penis inside of her and started to ride him slowly. She didn't expect him to cum again, she was just enjoying the feeling of him inside of her. As she moved up and down he started thrusting a little. Her hands were resting on his chest as she looked down at his face. He closed his eyes and bit his lower lip as she started to go faster. She was about to slide off and finish him with her mouth when he grabbed her hips and started thrusting harder and let out a loud grunt. He shuddered and stopped and his whole body slackened. She slid down on his chest, his cock still in her, and closed her eyes.

Her eyes opened with a start as she realized she had dozed off. His cock had slid out of her she moved off of him and settled in next to him. He was asleep. She looked at his penis and appreciated how nice it was and covered it with her hand and fell back asleep.

Chapter Thirty-Four

Kellie stared into the bathroom mirror as she applied her makeup. The moment she'd hoped for these past few months was almost here yet instead of being elated she was angry. Really angry. Angry at him for not accepting her the way she is. Angry at him for toying with her emotions, intentionally or not. Angry at him for walking out on her. Most of all she was angry at herself for allowing it all to happen. She was always so worried about pleasing without regard for her own needs. It wasn't his fault at all – it was hers. *This shit changes right now.*

She drove to the coffee shop where they were to meet but rather than arrive early as she always did she deliberately showed up ten minutes late. She assumed he was already there and parked around the side so he wouldn't see her pull up. She walked toward the entrance but stayed along the wall of the building to remain out of sight as long as possible. She spotted him looking out the window but in the opposite direction. She felt a pang in her chest and her stomach knotted up. He was glancing around nervously as if he was afraid she wouldn't show. She allowed herself a brief smile of satisfaction before returning to her stern expression and continued walking. *If he thinks this is going to be easy...*

Chet jumped up when she walked through the door, his face beaming. His smile vanished as he caught the cool glare she returned. He held out the chair as she walked over. They greeted each other for a brief hug. She sat down and looked at him and could tell he was a nervous wreck. *Go ahead, grovel.*

Chet cleared his throat. "I'm, I'm glad you came."

"It's been a long time."

"Too long, I'm sorry. I wanted to call you so many times."

"Why didn't you? I tried reaching out to you but you didn't bother to respond."

"I...I didn't know how...I wanted to. Kellie, I want you...I want you back."

Kellie didn't know what came over her. She knew what he wanted, she wanted it too, but she was getting satisfaction from seeing his angst. In an instant she realized how much pain he'd caused her, how much she suffered because of him. She loved him, there was no doubt about that, and she wanted him. But she knew the only way they would make it is if the dynamic of their relationship changed. Something Glenda said resonated with her now – "to find happiness you have to be assertive and take it, not wait for it." For most of her life she'd been the passive one and just accepted things as they were. *Be assertive.*

"What is it you want Chet? You want things to be like they were? You walked out on me – you *hurt* me."

Kellie looked at him as his eyes filled with tears, then started streaming down his face. She wanted to hold him and tell him everything would be okay but she knew she couldn't. It took all of her willpower to keep from breaking down herself. She held her tongue while he waited for her to continue.

She took a breath. "*If* I were to take you back things will be different."

"Anything, I'll do anything."

"First and foremost you will respect me and accept me for who I am."

"Of course," he said. "I've always respected you, you know that."

She ignored his comment. "Second, you will be conscious of my desires, not just your own. And that includes the desire to *not* do something, is that clear?"

"Yes, it's clear."

"Third you'll go to counseling with me."

"Counseling?" he asked. "You mean a shrink?"

"No, I've been seeing a sex therapist. Sex is not going to come between us anymore. We need to find a happy medium we can both be comfortable with. If that part of our relationship doesn't work nothing else will."

"Is there anything else?"

"Yes, you'll start by taking me on a date, a real dinner date."

His face brightened. "Sure, I'll pick a nice place."

"You'll take me to Andrè's."

"Andrè's? But that place is so –"

"You're taking me to Andrè's."

Chapter Thirty-Five

The sunlight streaming through the window reached Tracie's eyes waking her. Her head was resting on Steve's chest, her hand on his waist. She saw a bulge in the sheet and moved it aside to reveal his morning hard on. She brushed her fingertip across the tip causing it to twitch. Without moving her head she glanced upward to see that his eyes were still closed. Trying not to disturb him, she slid down so she could take him orally. She wrapped her fingers around the very thick shaft and brought her lips to him and took it in until it filled her mouth. She felt him stir.

"Ooohhh"

She worked his cock slowly, savoring every bit of it. One hand wrapped around and tugged lightly while the other gently massaged his balls. He shifted a little and she took advantage of his new position to allow her moistened finger to find his anus. Her mouth moved up and down slowly while her tongue worked the shaft and head. She pushed her finger into his ass and started working it in and out. He moaned softly.

She slid his penis out of her mouth but kept jerking him slowly by hand. Her finger still working his anus, she began to lick and suck his balls. She slid down further and pulled her finger out and used her hand to spread his cheeks. She used her tongue on his hole as he murmured a bit louder. He started to squirm and she saw his balls begin to tighten. She moved back up to take him in her mouth again. She started moving up and down at a faster pace as her finger returned to his ass. He moaned louder and started thrashing with his hands gripping the sheets tightly. Just as his body tensed she shoved her finger in his ass as far as it would go and took him deep into her mouth. He shuddered as a hot stream shot from his cock and hit the back of her throat. She didn't take her mouth off of him until she was sure she had taken every drop he had.

She climbed back to her position with her head on his chest as he tried to catch his breath. She looked at him and smiled. He was trying to say something but couldn't seem to form the words.

Tracie smiled. "Good morning."

"I...I..I have never, ever felt anything like that."

Tracie couldn't stop smiling as she drove to Kellie's house. She was wearing jeans and a pullover blouse having had the foresight to pack a change of clothes and keep them in her car. Steve sent the bellman to retrieve the bag for her so she wouldn't have to wear the dress home. They had room service breakfast and sat talking in a way that felt so comfortable. In her wildest fantasies she couldn't have imagined a night so perfect. Then it got better. He wanted to see her again and he wanted it to be soon. They agreed to meet that night in a much more relaxed fashion – beer and pizza.

She pulled into Kellie's driveway and walked up to the door. There was a note on it saying "come on in" so she walked inside. She found Kellie in the living room in her robe, her hair wrapped in a towel and one foot up on the coffee table as she was polishing her toenails.

Tracie threw her bag on the table. "I didn't know if that note was for me of your child-lover."

Kellie laughed. "I knew you'd be here any minute and I didn't want to have to get up and ruin the paint job. How did your date go?"

"I thought you'd never ask. It was unbelievable! The food was incredible and Steve was even better. Kellie, he looked in my eyes....my eyes!"

"So he looked in your eyes. What's the big deal about that?"

Tracie shook her head. "When I talk to guys I'm usually looking at the top of their head because their eyes are glued to my boobs."

Kellie laughed. "It's probably just the gravitational pull."

"No guy ever made me feel the way he did – and that was before we had sex."

Kellie switched feet and started polishing the other foot. "I hope you didn't do it right there in the restaurant."

Tracie told her about the hotel room and an extremely abbreviated version of her romp. By the time she was done Kellie had finished polishing and was resting both feet on the coffee table to let the toes dry. Through the afterglow of her night with Steve one dark cloud was trying to break through and it was the main reason she stopped by, she wanted her sister's advice though she knew what it was going to be.

Tracie shifted in her seat and leaned toward Kellie. "I don't know if I should tell him, about my lifestyle I mean."

"Do you like him? Are you planning to see him again?"

"Kellie, I think I'm in love."

"Holy shit. You *have* to tell him. He'll figure it out eventually."

"I know," Tracie said. "Damn it."

Tracie told her she was meeting him again that night and discussed the best way of breaking the news. They tossed around a few scenarios but kept coming back to just being totally honest as the best solution.

"So what's new with you?" Tracie finally asked. "Why all the primping?"

"I've got a date," she said. "With Chet."

"*What?* When did this happen?"

"He finally contacted me and we met for coffee. You'd be so proud of me; I didn't just go running back."

"Tell me everything."

"Well, Glenda said I needed to be more assertive and that I was responsible for my own happiness."

"I've been telling you that for years."

"But I'm paying her," Kellie said. "Anyway, I laid down the law and he agreed to everything. He's even going to go with me to see Glenda; I never thought he'd go along with that."

Tracie smiled. "Sis, he adores you, of course he would."

"I couldn't believe it was me talking. My god, he cried and I didn't!"

"And how did you feel afterward?"

"I almost peed my pants I was so nervous, and I'm not kidding. But it was like he wanted me to take charge."

Tracie laughed. "Like I told you, most guys like a strong woman who takes control."

Kellie thought of something else and blushed. "When I got home I was... I was so *horny*. I had to...I had to take care of myself right away. The weird thing is that was the third time I masturbated in a week, that's normally how often I do it in three months."

"Stop the presses! Sister Kellie of the order of prudes is waking up!"

"I hope so. I do need your advice, and I may need to borrow something from you."

Tracie was very surprised, even shocked by her sister's request. Still she told her everything she needed to know and wished her luck. Kellie had to get ready for her date so Tracie got up to go home.

Tracie stopped at the door. "So where is he taking you?"

"Andrè's"

"Wow, I got a peak at the bill last night. You know how much my dress cost, right? Well dinner was more than that."

"It's okay, I'm worth it."

"You go girl!"

Chapter Thirty-Six

Andrè's was busy but not crowded and Kellie absorbed the atmosphere determined to enjoy every moment of this. Chet was nervous and it showed, she was petrified but was able to put up a good front. After a couple of glasses of wine and some small talk they both started to relax. The ground rules were set early, no rehashing of what happened and no apologies. They were there to reconnect. Kellie loved him every bit as much as she always had but she could sense a shift, more in herself than him. She was no longer going to be a dutiful puppy dog, she was his partner. She felt empowered and she liked it. While she was petite in size she was feeling so much taller emotionally.

Taller or not, rather than lessen her inhibitions the couple of drinks made her doubt herself in regards to her ability to maintain the illusion of being totally in control. She was vulnerable by nature and one of the things she loved about Chet was that she could be vulnerable yet still feel safe. Therein lay the paradox – emotionally secure yet vulnerable, Kellie wanted it both ways. She needed him to see this part of her so he fully understood that it existed and that he had to respect it.

They finished dinner and declined desert but did sit for a while longer having coffee. Kellie saw Chet's expression turn serious. He reached his hand across the table and covered hers and gave it a gentle squeeze.

"I am so happy to be here with you," he said.

"I'm happy too."

He leaned forward a little. "I...I was hoping I could move back in."

He heart pounded, it was what she wanted too. "Not just yet, I'm afraid."

"I understand, but I didn't want there to be any doubt."

She moved her free hand over so she held his in both of hers. "This is what has to happen, we keep going on dates and we complete Glenda's program."

"Glenda?"

"The therapist we're going to see."

His face clouded. "How long is that?"

"I think it's eight or ten weeks. If that goes well you can propose to me when it's done."

"Propose?"

"Yes, propose. And it better be good, I'm very picky."

He laughed. "So I've heard."

"Now take me home, but don't get any ideas. Don't expect me to put out just because you bought me dinner, I'm not that kind of girl."

Chapter Thirty-Seven

The pub was packed with the typical Saturday night crowd. They ate pizza at Tracie's favorite Italian restaurant and now moved to the bar in the same shopping center. They picked up right where they left off the night before. They had so much in common. They liked the same kind of food, music, movies, books and TV shows. Steve loved to travel and had been all over the world and loved talking about what he'd seen. So many of the destinations were ones Tracie was dying to visit. She was so wrapped up in the conversation that she almost forgot what she really had to talk about. Almost.

She didn't want to discuss it over dinner figuring that it would be easier after a couple of beers. Now she was thinking of excuses to put it off even longer. She dropped a few hints hoping he might give her an opening but he never did. She suggested a round of shots thinking it would give her the courage to tell him. If she didn't like him it wouldn't matter. But she did like him – a lot. This was one of the rare times that she found her lifestyle to be inconvenient but she still made no apologies for it. She just hoped her wouldn't walk out on her.

The waitress came over with two shots of tequila along with lime wedges. The two of them did the ritual with the salt and lime and downed the shot in one gulp. Tracie shuddered as the booze burned her throat on the way down. She thought about having another.

Steve looked her in the eye. "Are you going to tell me what's bothering you?"

"What do you mean?"

"You've been acting strange ever since we got here. Did I order the wrong topping for the pizza?"

Tracie laughed."No, of course not."

"Well, you couldn't know if you were pregnant yet and I can say with absolutely certainty that you aren't really a man. So let me guess, you're in the witness protection program."

"No, nothing so exciting."

"Then the only thing left that it could possibly be is that you're a dominatrix who enjoys spanking men."

Tracie was speechless as her mouth hung agape. This is not something someone could randomly guess. Did Kellie tell him? No, she wouldn't do that. Did they have a common friend who knew of her fetish?

"How...how did you come to that?"

Steve smiled. "A little detective work –emphasis on little – and a few mouse clicks. I was smitten, as they say, from the minute I saw you. So I did a little digging."

"The moment you saw me? *Really?*"

"Yes, from the moment I met you," he said. "I saw you on Kellie's Facebook friends list so I clicked on your profile. There was a link to your *Fetlife* profile so I clicked that and, well, wow."

"You saw my *Fetlife* page?"

"Yup"

"And you knew this *before* you asked me out?"

"Yup"

"And you're okay with it?"

"Would I have asked you out if I wasn't?"

Tracie shook her head in amazement. "I don't know what to say. I read people pretty well and I *never* pegged you as a guy who liked to be dominated."

Steve laughed. "I'm not at all."

"I'm confused. Then why the interest in *me*?"

"You mean besides the fact that you're smart, funny, beautiful, tall, and have just enough meat on your bones? And let's not forget that you don't shave your bush, though it needs to fill in a little more."

Tracie beamed. "Beautiful? You think I'm beautiful?"

"Young lady, you are fucking *gorgeous*!"

"Really? Seriously though, if you don't like to be dommed..."

"Steve's voice got firm."I want a strong woman and one who isn't afraid to push the envelope and try new things. I want a woman who gives as good as she gets, and believe me you give pretty good."

"Wow"

"All that being said, you've been pretty naughty and I think *you're* the one who needs to be taught a lesson with a good spanking."

"*You're* going to spank *me*?"

"Yup"

Tracie was giggling. "We'll see about that. How about naked wrestling? First one pinned gets spanked."

"Deal," Steve said.

"Let's get out of here before I cum in my pants."

They left and as they were walking to the car Tracie couldn't stop laughing.

"What's so funny?" he asked.

"I guess you didn't know I was the state wrestling champ in high school."

Steve smirked. "I took the bronze in Greco-Roman wrestling at the ninety-six Olympics in Atlanta."

"Oh, shit."

Chapter Thirty-Eight

The car pulled into Kellie's driveway. He looked over at her but she just stared straight ahead. He moved toward her but she turned away and looked out the window. When he didn't get the message she looked back at him.

"A gentleman walks a lady to her door he doesn't kick her out at the curb."

"Right"

Chet walked around top the passenger side and opened the door for her. He followed her up the steps to the front door. She put her key in the lock and pushed the door open and stepped inside while he stayed on the steps.

She looked back at him. "Well, are you coming in?"

He hesitated a second longer before stepping inside. "I'm sorry, you confuse me."

She turned away as her mouth turned upward in a sly smile. She knew it wouldn't last but at least for now he was on his toes. She told him to have a seat then went into the kitchen and poured a glass of wine for each of them. She came back into the living room, handed him his glass and sat on the adjacent couch. When she kicked off her shoes and curled her legs up on the couch her skirt rode up past her knee exposing the top of her thigh drawing his gaze right to it. She spotted a growing bulge in his pants and wondered if he was bold enough to make a move or if she had scared him too much to try.

They sat drinking their wine and chatting about inconsequential things. It was clear he wasn't going to do anything so it would be up to her to make something happen. She knew he wanted sex. She wanted to connect so they could get past this tension and though she didn't need it, she knew sex was the way to clear the air. She put her glass down and moved to the bedroom. He didn't follow so she just took her clothes off and went back to the doorway.

She stood there naked. "Are you going to make love to me or not?"

He almost spilled what was left of his wine in his haste to get up. He was unbuttoning his shirt by the time her reached the doorway and she moved to help him. He bent down to kiss her and they moved toward the bed with their lips locked and tongues probing. He clumsily removed his pants and underwear and they fell onto the bed on their sides. They kept kissing as he rubbed his erection against her thigh. He nudged her to get her to lie on her back but she pushed him until her was the one face up. She straddled his stomach and brought her boobs down so he could suck her nipples.

"God I've missed them," he said.

When her nipples were good and hard she moved up until her pussy was in his face. Her hands held the headboard for support as his tongue licked her clit. She started bucking slowly as he ate her. She closed her eyes and tossed her head back and did something she almost never did – she allowed herself to get lost in the feeling. Her legs started to quiver and an electric jolt coursed through her causing her thighs to spasm.

"Argghh!"

She pulled herself away from his mouth and slid down still straddling him. She moved until she felt the tip of his cock and was about to reach back to guide him but she was so wet he just slipped right in. He let out a low moan as her fingers interlaced with his, both their hands next to his head. She started to move slowly and quickened her pace until she was moving in a nice rhythm. She felt another orgasm building, another rarity for her. It was close as he started to breathe heavier and his body shuddered with his ejaculation. She kept going until she came again and then collapsed on top of him. His arms went around her as they both caught their breath.

"That was awesome," Chet said. "I love it with you on top like that."

"Mmmm, it *was* fun."

Kellie hugged him tight, she missed being close to him. The crazy idea she had talked to Tracie about ran through her head and she realized she never could have pulled it off. How did she even think it was possible? *Bat-shit crazy*. He rolled away from her so she sat up wrapped in the sheet and hugging her knees to her chest. Chet sat up next to her.

He looked at her. "I feel like such a shit for the way I treated you, you deserve so much better."

She wrapped an arm around his and leaned her head on his shoulder. "Look, it happened. We'll fix this. I was hurt, but I'm not mad at you."

"How can you forgive me?"

"Don't worry, I do."

"But I can't forgive myself," he said.

"Don't dwell on it."

"I just wish there was something that would make it go away. Do my penance, pay for my transgression and feel better."

Kellie let go of him and pulled away. She thought about it for a minute and then got out of the bed and stood facing him.

"Do you mean that?" she asked.

"Of course I do."

Kellie took her robe out of the closet, put it on and tied it tight. She went through the living room towards the coat closet and retrieved what she was looking for. She walked back to the bedroom and stopped a few feet from the bed. He sat there looking at her trying to figure out what she was holding behind her back.

"Get out of bed."

"Why?"

"Just do it!"

"Okay, okay."

He stood there naked about two feet away from her and waited.

"Get on your hands and knees."

"What? Why?"

"Do it!"

"Okay, I'm doing it."

Chet dropped to his knees and put his hands palm-down on the floor. Kellie walked behind him so he couldn't see what she was doing. She brought the ten-inch wooden paddle she borrowed from Tracie from behind her back and gave his ass a firm, but not too hard, smack.

"Hey, what was that?"

"You wanted to be punished, you're being punished so shut up and take it."

Chet maintained his position only moving his knees apart for better balance. She hit him again, a little harder this time. Tracie was right, the paddle gave a small girl like her much better leverage and didn't hurt her hand at all. She hit him a little harder.

"Ow"

Whack

He gritted his teeth and she could see he was trying not to cry out. She swung harder still.

Whack

"Ow"

Whack

"urgghh"

She was moving around and about to stop when she saw he had an erection, a massive erection. I'm *beating his ass and he likes it, he likes it!*

Whack!

His ass was glowing red but he was smiling and he had a hard-on. *Bat-shit crazy.*

Kellie finally stopped because she was exhausted. She sat on the edge of the bed and told him to get up. He moved slowly but the erection remained. She motioned for him to stand in front of her. She looked at his cock, really looked at it. She held it in her hand and felt it. She pulled him closer and touched the tip with her tongue. She didn't recoil or feel the need to retch. She hesitated for a second, opened her mouth and took it in a few inches. She instantly felt that he was bigger that the toy dick she got from cock class.

Chet cooed softly. She took it in a little further. When she realized she wasn't gagging on it she started slowly moving up and down and using her tongue a little. This isn't so bad. She was just starting to get into it when she felt his hand on the back of her head. She pulled off of him and in a swift motion shoved his hand aside.

"Don't you ever, ever do that to me."

He moved his hand away and she started again. He started to moan a little. She knew she wasn't doing it that well and nicked him with her teeth a couple of times but he didn't seem to mind at all. He did have a big cock and she had a small mouth so it wasn't so easy. She began to move a little quicker and he started to shift a bit. She had one hand on his balls and felt them getting tighter. She remembered from class that this was a signal that he was about to ejaculate. She pulled her mouth off of him and started jerking him by hand. As she did he grunted and shot a load over her shoulder and onto the bed. She wrapped her arms around him and hugged him close.

"That...that was awesome."

"The blowjob or the spanking?"

"Both"

Kellie smiled. "Good, now go home."

Epilogue

It was a beautiful Sunday morning though it was supposed to be fairly hot by afternoon. Kellie was preparing some cantaloupe, strawberries and grapefruit. Muffins were baking in the oven and bagels were sliced and on the table. Coffee was brewing and the cream cheese, butter and assorted jams were ready and waiting in the fridge. She looked at the clock just as the doorbell rang. She went to answer but Tracie had already let herself in.

"Hi Kellie, you're looking radiant this morning. I guess the date went well?"

Kellie beamed. "You have no idea."

Tracie started helping out by arranging plates on the table. She was wearing loose-fitting shorts and a tight top that was straining to contain her boobs. Kellie was noticing her sister's sandals when she spotted a nasty bruise forming on her thigh and another darker mark on the back of her left bicep.

Kellie pointed at Tracie's leg. "That looks like it hurts. What happened?"

"Wrestling accident."

Kellie let it go, afraid of what the details might be. "Everything's ready, we just need our guests to arrive. Why don't you have a seat?"

"I think I'll be standing for a bit."

The doorbell rang and Tracie went to answer it. She returned a moment later arm-in-arm with Chet.

"Look who I found," Tracie said.

Chet released Tracie and walked over to Kellie and gave her a kiss. She hugged him and returned to the counter to retrieve the coffee pot. Tracie took it from her and set it down on the dining room table, leaving her sister and Chet alone.

Chet came up behind Kellie and put his arms around her and nibbled her earlobe. "I love you so much."

Kellie shivered and turned to kiss him just as his hand cupped her breast. "Behave yourself."

"And if I don't?"

"You'll get punished," she said. "And you won't get the treat I have planned for you."

"Decisions, decisions," Chet said. "Do I want the treat or the punishment?"

Kellie laughed and pushed him away just as Tracie walked back into the kitchen. The doorbell chimed again and Tracie rushed to answer it. Chet and Kellie went into the dining room as Steve was walking in. He handed Kellie a bottle of wine and kissed her on the cheek. She took the bottle and moved to the counter to find a corkscrew and open it. She moved back to the dining room and saw the three of them chatting. He sister was hanging onto Steve and leaning her head on his shoulder. She watched as Steve slid his hand down to her ass and gave her cheek a light squeeze causing a visible wince from Tracie. She had to bite her tongue to keep from laughing. *Looks like she's met her match.*

Steve looked toward Kellie. "I hope it's okay but I told Jason to come over. Tracie wanted to meet him."

"Of course, it'll be nice to see him again."

Tracie gave her an evil grin. "And for him to *see* you I'm sure."

Kellie shot a glance at her sister but smiled and ignored the remark. She sat down as did Steve but Tracie and Chet remained standing.

Steve pulled out a chair and gestured to Steve to sit. "Thanks, but I think I'll be standing for a while."

Tracie's eyes went wide as she glanced from Kellie, to Steve, and back to her sister again. Kellie felt the heat rising in her face as it turned crimson. She was afraid her sister was going to say something embarrassing but she was saved by the bell – literally. Chet moved to the door and opened it for Jason and introduced himself. Steve then introduced him to Tracie and Jason greeted Kellie.

Tracie extended her hand and when Jason went to shake it she pulled him in for a hug. "I've heard so much about you; it's a pleasure to finally meet you. Although I understand you've *seen* quite a bit of my sister already."

Kellie wanted to kill her, instead she addressed to group. "You should see the terrific job Jason did in the yard, it looks fabulous."

They all went out back to take a look. Chet seemed impressed and Kellie was relieved. The yard had been his baby and someone else had finished it though that didn't seem to bother him at all. They moved back inside and had a bit more to eat and sat around the table talking. Kellie started to clear the empty plates and Tracie helped her. They were alone in the kitchen when Tracie came over to her.

"You look so happy," Tracie said.

A tear rolled down Kellie's cheek. "I am."

Tracie hugged her and wiped away the tear. She kissed her on the cheek and went back to the dining room. Kellie started to follow but stopped because her sundress had gotten a bit loose. She reached behind her neck to untie and refasten it. She was fumbling with it when the straps slipped from her hand. She tried to grab them but missed and the top slipped down exposing her right breast just as the door opened.

"Ms. Boyd, I'm leav..." Jason's eyes opened wide.

She quickly covered herself. "I'm sorry Jason; I'm always doing that to you."

"I don't mind, really...I mean it's —"

She held her dress up with one hand and put the other arm around him. "Say no more and *you're* not the one who should be embarrassed, it's our little secret." *Bat-shit crazy!*

Jason left while Kellie pulled herself back together. She returned to the dining room to find Chet standing there alone. He helped her put the rest of the stuff away. She assumed Tracie and Steve were outside saying goodbye to Jason.

*****

When Jason left Tracie grabbed Steve's hand and put a finger to her lips to keep him quiet. He gave her a quizzical look but she just pulled him along. They moved down the hallway to Kellie's bedroom and entered silently. Tracie gently closed the door and locked it. While Steve looked on she moved to Kellie's dresser and looked around. She spotted a ceramic dish with an assortment of rings on it. She carefully put the rings on the dresser and turned to Steve signaling him to come to her. When he did she dropped to her knees and unzipped him. Her fingers tugged his underwear down so she could get at his cock. By the time she had it in her mouth he was already hard. After sucking for a few seconds she stood up and started jerking him.

"I need you to cum really fast."

He turned his back to the dresser, closed his eyes and used his hands to brace himself by placing them palms-down on the top. Tracie jerked faster and held the dish up to his cock. Tracie saw a drop of semen on the tip and watched his legs start to quiver. Steve grunted a bit as he ejaculated onto the dish with some of his semen landing on her hand. When he was done she put the dish on top of the dresser and licked her hand clean. As he was putting himself back together Tracie found a piece of paper and a pen and wrote something down, leaving the note next to the dish.

*****

Kellie heard footsteps and saw Steve and Tracie returning to the dining room. She'd been talking to Chet and had totally forgotten about them. Tracie came up to her and gave her a hug.

"We're going to be heading out," Tracie said. "What are you guys doing the rest of the day?"

Kellie looked at Chet then at Tracie. "We're going to the mall."

"The *mall*?" Chet said.

"Trust me – you're going to like it."

Tracie and Steve left and Kellie told Chet she would be ready to go in a minute. She went down the hall and into her bedroom. She quickly removed her sundress and threw it on the bed. She retrieved another one from the closet, Chet's favorite, and put it on. She looked at herself in the mirror for a moment. Then she pulled the dress up and removed her panties and tossed them on the bed. She turned around, leaned forward a little and pulled the dress up exposing her bare ass. She looked at herself for a moment and smiled. *Bat-shit crazy!*

She was about to leave when she spotted the note on her dresser. She picked it up and saw one word written in her sister's handwriting – *payback*. She laughed out loud and dropped the note. She saw the dish next to it with a gooey substance on it. She dipped her fingertip in it and brought it to her nose to sniff. Her finger returned to the dish and picked up a bigger gob which she brought to her mouth and hesitated before licking it clean.

"Mmmm, yummy!"

About the Author

J.W. Richard is a freelance journalist and a graduate of the University of Nevada Las Vegas. Originally from New York, J.W. currently resides in Las Vegas, Nevada.

www.jwrichard.com